Will Ashleigh's past stand in the way of Christina's future?

Christina blinked back tears of anger and frustration. Star was her horse, and her opinion should count when it came to his training. "Maybe my tension isn't the problem," she snapped at her mother. "Maybe you just don't want him to succeed."

Ashleigh's face paled, and she stared at Christina in shock. "What are you talking about?" she asked.

"You've always resented him," Christina said, fighting not to cry. "You blamed him for Wonder dying. You sent him to Townsend Acres so you wouldn't have to have anything to do with him. You don't care about Star and the Derby. You probably want to see him lose!"

Before her mother could say anything in response, Christina fled the office. She stormed from the barn and hurried toward the house, her mind churning. Star needed a chance to run hard, and he needed to do it soon. If her mother wouldn't let her work Star the way he needed, maybe she'd have to start training him on her own, secretly.

Collect all the books in the Thoroughbred series

Collect all the books in the Ashleigh series

coming soon*

THOROUGHBRED

DERBY FEVER

CREATED BY
JOANNA CAMPBELL

WRITTEN BY
MARY ANDERSON

HarperEntertainment
An Imprint of HarperCollinsPublishers

♜ HarperEntertainment
An Imprint of HarperCollins*Publishers*
10 East 53rd Street, New York, NY 10022-5299

This is a work of fiction. The characters, incidents, and dialogues are products of the author's imagination and are not to be construed as real. Any resemblance to actual events or persons, living or dead, is entirely coincidental.

Produced by 17th Street Productions, an Alloy Online, Inc., company

HarperCollins books are available at special quantity discounts for bulk purchases for sales promotions, premiums, or fund-raising. For information please call or write: Special Markets Department, HarperCollins Publishers Inc., 10 East 53rd Street, New York, NY 10022-5299. Telephone: (212) 207-7528. Fax: (212) 207-7222.

ISBN 0-06-106823-3

Cover art © 2002 by 17th Street Productions, an Alloy Online, Inc., company

First printing: June 2002

Printed in the United States of America

Visit HarperEntertainment on the World Wide Web at
www.harpercollins.com

❖ 10 9 8 7 6 5 4 3 2 1

For my very cool mom, Rosellen Newhall, with love.
Thanks for keeping me in horses and
for all the writing inspiration.

"Whoa, Star!" Christina Reese exclaimed, laughing as she pulled back on the reins. Wonder's Star, her chestnut Thoroughbred colt, tossed his head, straining against the pressure on his bit as he fought to break into a gallop. Eighteen-year-old Christina restrained the eager colt as they circled the practice track at Whitebrook, the Thoroughbred breeding and training farm owned by Christina's parents.

On a knoll overlooking the track stood the family's old white farmhouse. As far as Christina could see, white fences surrounded vast pastures of Kentucky bluegrass. She and Star jogged around the curve of the track, and Whitebrook's expansive barns came into view.

Star tried to snatch the bit and break into a run again, but Christina hauled on the reins. "I mean it this time, boy," she said, putting her weight firmly on the colt's back. "It's time to cool down."

Christina would have loved to let Star gallop, but her mother had given strict instructions to keep the colt's workout slow and easy. Christina finally slowed Star to an energetic walk, giving him a chance to settle down before she ended his work.

As they neared the gap in the track's rail, Christina saw her mother, Ashleigh Griffen, nodding in approval. Christina patted Star's neck, which was only slightly damp with sweat. "He's dying to run," she said, bringing the colt to a stop.

Ashleigh caught Star's headstall, holding the colt still while Christina jumped from his tall back. "I can see that," she said. "As good as he looks right now, he'll scare the other horses right off the track at Churchill Downs on Kentucky Derby day."

Christina pulled Star's saddle from his back. "Maybe we should race him once before the Derby," she suggested. "It would sure prove to the world that he's in perfect condition to run for the roses."

Ashleigh shook her head slowly. "I don't think that's a good idea," she said.

Christina was about to press her mom for an explanation when Dani Martens, one of Whitebrook's part-time grooms, came out to the track holding a cooling sheet and Star's halter.

"I'll walk him out for you, Chris," Dani said as she threw the light blanket over Star's back. "I don't have any classes this morning, and I know you need to get ready for school." Dani, a student at the local college, was studying to be a veterinarian. Christina was still finishing her senior year at Henry Clay High School.

"Thanks, Dani," Christina said gratefully. She gave Star's neck an affectionate rub and quickly kissed the colt's soft nose. Now that she was standing still, she felt the chill of the morning air seep through her light jacket, and she shivered.

"Are you cold?" Ashleigh asked.

"Just a little," Christina admitted.

"You got used to that balmy California weather," Dani said, chuckling. Christina had recently returned from a stay in southern California, where she had taken Star for additional training and to run at the Santa Anita track. "Do you miss the palm trees and orange groves?"

"I'm not that cold," Christina said quickly. "And I'll take bluegrass over palm trees any day." She glanced at Star, who pawed impatiently at the ground, then raised his head and snorted. "Star's glad to be

3

home, too," she added, patting the colt's neck. "I'll see you this afternoon, big guy," she said, then watched Dani walk the muscular colt away before she turned back to her mother. "So I still don't understand—*why* shouldn't we race Star again before the Derby?" she asked.

Ashleigh picked up a clipboard she had propped against the bottom rail surrounding the practice track and started making notes about Star's work. "He's definitely in top form," she said. "But I just don't think we should push him. He needs to save his endurance and speed for the Derby."

"But, Mom—" Christina started to protest.

Ashleigh raised her hand to cut her daughter off. "No buts," she said, then glanced at her watch. "You'll be late for school if you don't get moving," she said. "We'll discuss Star's schedule later, okay?"

"Fine," Christina agreed reluctantly. She turned and strode toward the house as Ashleigh headed for the barn and her office.

Why won't she let us run another race? Christina asked herself as she hurried to the house. *Doesn't she see how ready he is to run?* She took a quick shower, dressed, and dried her long red-brown hair, then grabbed her schoolbooks and headed out the door. As she started to climb into the Blazer she co-owned with her cousin, Melanie Graham, she heard someone call her name. Christina paused at the Blazer's open door and looked over her shoulder.

Kevin McLean was jogging up the path from his family's cottage, waving frantically. "Wait up," Kevin called. "I need a ride."

Kevin's father, Ian McLean, was Whitebrook's head trainer, so Christina and Kevin had grown up together on the Thoroughbred farm, and the lanky redhead was like a brother to her. Although he was a skilled horseman, Kevin had turned his focus from riding to playing soccer and planned to attend college on a sports scholarship.

"I'm glad I caught you," Kevin said when he reached the Blazer. "I missed the bus and Mom has to work this morning, so I can't use her car." Beth McLean taught aerobics at a gym in nearby Lexington. All the McLeans were athletic, just like Christina's family.

"Hop in," Christina said, climbing into the driver's seat.

Kevin settled in on the passenger side, then glanced at Christina and tilted his head to the side. "What's the big scowl for, Reese?" he asked.

"I'm not scowling," Christina said quickly. She put the SUV in gear and headed down the driveway, then let out a deep sigh. "I'm just trying to figure out why Mom thinks Star doesn't have it in him to run another race before the Kentucky Derby."

Kevin smiled. "Don't you trust your mom's judgment when it comes to training racehorses?" he asked.

"Of course I do," she said. She pressed her lips together, her frustration building. "But this is different. I know Star, and I know he's ready to run now."

Kevin shrugged. "Good luck convincing Ashleigh," he said. "If she doesn't want Star to race, you know she's got a good reason."

"I just don't see what it would be," Christina grumbled.

Kevin didn't respond, and they were both silent as they drove the rest of the way to Henry Clay High School.

"So I guess I'll see you later, Kev," Christina said as she pulled into a spot in the student parking lot.

"Yeah, try to have a good day," Kevin said. He jumped out and headed for his first-period class.

By afternoon, Christina had worked out a detailed argument in her head to convince her mother that being overly cautious wasn't in Star's best interest. Ashleigh had to see that Star had plenty of fire and really needed another race to stay geared up for the Derby. Not letting him compete would be disheartening for the colt.

Christina couldn't wait to get home and plead her case. But she had to stay after school to make up a test she had missed while she was in California, so it was late in the afternoon by the time she headed for Whitebrook.

Although the morning had been clear and dry, rain had started to fall before school let out. The farms she drove past looked like watercolor paintings. Blurred by the rainfall, most of the rolling pastures were empty. She knew the dozens of horses she usually saw were in the sprawling barns, staying warm and dry.

She finally pulled into her driveway, gearing up to change her mother's mind about letting Star race soon. Just like the farms she had driven past, Whitebrook's pastures were empty of horses. Christina stopped the Blazer at the house and went inside to change into old jeans and a barn jacket, then hurried down to the barn.

She burst into Ashleigh's office without knocking, but her mother wasn't there. She stood there a second, looking around the room in disappointment. Then she realized her mother was probably over in the yearling barn, looking over the colts and fillies with Ian. But she stopped at the barn doorway, gazing out at the falling rain for a minute, listening to the familiar, comforting sound of rustling hay and the occasional swish of a tail or stomp of a hoof. Inhaling deeply, Christina took in the rich smells of the horses and the barn, then turned and strolled down the barn aisle, stopping at a few stalls where the horses lifted their heads to eye her.

"Hello, Catwink," she said when she reached the gray filly's stall. Catwink sniffed at Christina's jacket, but when she realized Christina wasn't bringing her extra grain or offering her a treat, the filly turned her attention back to her hay net. Christina walked on, stopping at the next filly's stall. Raven bobbed her black head and nickered softly, letting Christina pet her sleek neck before she returned to her food.

When Christina neared Star's stall, the colt poked his red-brown head into the aisle, his bright eyes looking in her direction. He whinnied loudly and stomped his foot impatiently.

Christina hurried to the stall. She rubbed the colt's sleek neck as she glanced over the stall door at the hay net hanging in one corner. "You haven't even touched your hay," she said with a frown. "What's the matter, boy?" Star shoved his nose at her and grunted softly. Christina rubbed the white star on his forehead.

"I'll be right back with a brush and currycomb," she told him. "Maybe after a nice grooming you'll settle down and eat." She hurried to the tack room and in a minute was back at Star's stall, grooming kit in hand.

The colt nudged her as she let herself into the stall, then snuffled at her pockets. "Oh, you want dessert before you eat the main course," she said, laughing as she dug a chunk of carrot from her jacket.

Star crunched the treat noisily as Christina set her grooming tools down. When she started to straighten, Star gave her another nudge, nearly pushing her over.

"Stop that!" she exclaimed, turning to push the colt's nose back. "You're way too big to be shoving me around, and you know better. Where are your manners?"

Star raised his head, pricked his ears, and widened his eyes, looking shocked at the tone of Christina's voice. She shook her finger at him. "You behave, big guy," she said, the fondness in her voice belying her stern expression. Star bobbed his head, then craned his neck toward her, sniffing at her hands.

"Yes, I love you, too," Christina said as she began massaging his neck. Star sighed with pleasure as she worked the rubber currycomb along the muscles that rippled under his glossy coat. With only a month before the Derby, making sure that he stayed fit and healthy was one of her biggest concerns. The Kentucky Derby would be the biggest race of their lives, and she wanted them both to be in perfect shape.

"He sure does look great."

Christina glanced up at the sound of Dani's voice and flashed her a smile. Dani stopped at the stall, an empty wheelbarrow in front of her.

"Yeah, he does look great," Christina agreed. "He's ready to race again," she added. "I think it would be good to run him in one more race before the Derby, but Mom wants to keep him on light works so he'll be ready to go in May."

"That makes sense," Dani said.

Christina tried to restrain a groan. First Kevin, now Dani. Did everyone always agree with her mother? "I'm afraid he's getting bored with all the rest and relaxation, though," she pressed, looking the colt over again. Star shifted his weight and struck at the stall floor, digging a furrow in the thick bedding under his hooves.

"See what I mean?" Christina asked. "He's getting antsy. He needs to run."

Dani shrugged. "Your mother is a great trainer," she said. "I'm sure she knows what she's doing."

Christina nodded slowly. "I know," she said, still not at all sure that her mother's training program was what the energetic colt needed just then.

"You're probably both a little edgy with the pressure of such a big race ahead of you," Dani pointed out, giving Christina a reassuring smile.

"Maybe that's it," Christina agreed. She was excited about racing Star in the Derby, but every time she thought of the prestigious race she felt herself tense up. Winning the race would be a wonderful thing—for Star, for her, and for Whitebrook as well. She couldn't help feeling that she'd be letting a lot of people down if she and Star didn't give their best performance there.

"Well, I guess I'll see you later," Dani said, grabbing the handles of her wheelbarrow. "I have mountains of homework tonight. I'm taking two science classes this quarter."

"That sounds like fun," Christina commented. She gave Dani another smile before the other girl walked away, then returned her attention to Star. After giving him a thorough brushing with a soft finishing brush, she ran her hands along his flanks, feeling the faint bumps of his ribs beneath his shiny coat. She frowned, then put on her sternest gaze and pointed at his hay net.

"Eat," she said. But Star tossed his head as if to say no, and Christina's frown deepened. Finally she gave his long, graceful neck a pat. "I'm going to leave you alone. Maybe if you get tired of just standing around you'll finish your dinner." Star nuzzled at her pockets again, smacking his lips as he searched for more carrot bits. Christina dug one more piece out of her pocket and fed it to him.

"You can't live on carrots," she said firmly. "But I'll talk to Mom about your feed rations," she added as she opened the stall door. "Maybe you need a different kind of hay."

As she started to leave, Star pawed at his bedding again and tossed his head, then pranced in place for a moment. Christina sighed. "You really are getting tired of standing around so much, aren't you? You need something challenging to keep you occupied." She latched the stall door, pausing to give the colt's sleek nose a final stroke. "I'll make sure Mom understands," she promised, then went in search of her mother.

Christina knew Ashleigh was a top expert when it came to racehorses. Ashleigh's racing and training experience had helped elevate Whitebrook's small operation to the status of some of the legendary old Thoroughbred farms in Kentucky. Ashleigh, along with Christina's father, Mike Reese, and their head trainer, Ian McLean, had worked hard to gain a reputation for breeding and training some of the finest racehorses in the country.

Christina respected her mother's knowledge and skill in training racehorses, and she rarely questioned Ashleigh's expertise. But she still felt that Star needed something more than light jogging on the farm's practice track to keep his mind and body fit for the upcoming Derby.

The barn office was still empty, so Christina sat down at the desk. She glanced at the training schedules and old copies of the *Daily Racing Form* stacked on one corner of the desk, but there was nothing new. She'd already seen the articles written about Star and Gratis, another Derby contender that she had ridden several times. She'd also read about Celtic Mist, the third horse with a good chance at the Derby. Celtic Mist was owned by Townsend Acres, the same farm that had produced Star's dam, Ashleigh's Wonder. Christina just hoped that when it came down to it, she and Star would have what it took to beat Gratis and Celtic Mist.

Finally Christina leaned back and gazed at the photo-covered walls. Some of the pictures showed Whitebrook horses racing, while others displayed the farm's horses in the winner's circles of almost every track on the East Coast.

Her gaze settled on one of her on Star at Churchill Downs the previous spring. She was wearing Whitebrook's blue-and-white silks. The twin spires of the grandstand were in the background. The expression of joy on her face made Christina smile. Winning that race had been a turning point for her and Star. After a difficult birth that had taken the life of his dam, Wonder, Christina had struggled to keep the sickly foal alive. Her mother, traumatized by the loss of her beloved Wonder, had sent Star to Townsend Acres to be trained as a racehorse.

But after a poor start, the Reeses had brought him back to Whitebrook, where Christina worked daily with the colt to get him ready to race. Then a mysterious virus had almost taken Star's life. His comeback in racing was nothing short of a miracle. The fact that he was going to race in the Kentucky Derby said a lot about Star's talent and spirit. Christina felt her heart swell with love for the chestnut colt.

"What are you looking so pleased about?" Christina nearly jumped, then turned her head to see Ashleigh standing in the office doorway.

"I was just thinking about Star," Christina said, hopping out of her mother's chair.

Ashleigh pulled off her wet jacket, then gathered her loose hair into a ponytail and dug a rubber band from her pocket to hold the handful of hair. Christina marveled again at the way her petite mother didn't look any older now than she must have all those years ago when she had raced Wonder as a three-year-old. The jeans, sweatshirt, and casual hairdo made her seem more like Christina's sister than her mother.

Ashleigh nodded at the photo of Star and Christina hanging on the wall. "He's pretty amazing," she said. "I'm looking forward to seeing the two of you race in the Derby."

"I'm excited, too," Christina said, but there was a little catch in her voice.

"What is it?" Ashleigh asked, picking up on her daughter's emotions right away, as she always did. "Are you getting nervous about the big race?"

"No!" Christina exclaimed. "Not at all. I think Star is going to be fantastic. Well, I mean, I think he will be if we give him a chance to get out some energy in advance. Mom, he's ready to run now. Why do we have to wait so long to let him race again?"

"Honey, I'm sorry," Ashleigh replied. "The timing is just too tricky. It would be different if the Derby weren't so close, but I don't want to run him hard just a few weeks before the race, considering the medical problems he's had. Remember, it was only a few months ago that we almost lost him to that terrible virus, Chris. So we'll just keep doing maintenance workouts and not stress him. I expect by Derby day he'll be more than ready to blow away the rest of the field."

Christina was ready to scream. Why wouldn't her

mother listen to her? Christina knew Star was in perfect health. Whatever had made him sick was long gone, and she didn't think there was any way it was coming back.

"He's getting tired of not doing anything," she argued. "He's in great shape right now. Do you really think another race between now and the Derby would be too much?" She held her breath, waiting for her mother's response.

Ashleigh furrowed her brow. "I thought about it, Chris," she admitted. "I talked it over with Ian, too. He agrees that having Star take it easy is the best plan. I don't want to risk a relapse after how ill Star was, or work him into an injury. I think we're better off being a little cautious."

"He's perfectly sound and healthy," Christina maintained. "You saw him run at Santa Anita, Mom. Star is in top form right now. And he's getting bored with the easy riding you're having us do."

Ashleigh angled her head and gazed at Christina for a moment. "Maybe you should start taking him out on the trails," she suggested. "Just stay on the well-groomed paths and keep it down to a light jog."

"What he really wants is to get on the track and run hard," Christina said. "I can feel it when I'm working him."

"Good," Ashleigh said. "That means by Derby time he'll be more than ready. For now we need to keep his track sessions to a minimum."

Christina started to protest again, but Ashleigh raised her hand and gave Christina a firm look. "Give me some credit for knowing how to train a Derby winner, Chris."

"But he's off his feed," Christina protested. "He's wound up and too edgy to eat. He needs to blow off some steam, Mom."

Ashleigh looked at her thoughtfully. "Maybe he's wound up because you are," she said. "This pre-Derby time is very stressful for all of us. You need to be careful not to let Star feed off your tension, okay?"

Christina blinked back tears of anger and frustration. Star was her horse, and her opinion should count when it came to his training. "Maybe it isn't my tension," she snapped, glaring at her mother. "Maybe you just don't want him to succeed."

Ashleigh's face paled, and she stared at Christina in shock. "What are you talking about?" she asked.

"You've always resented him," Christina said, fighting not to cry. "You blamed him for Wonder dying. You sent him to Townsend Acres so you wouldn't have to have anything to do with him. You don't care about Star and the Derby. You probably want to see him lose!"

Before her mother could say anything in response, Christina fled the office. She stormed from the barn and hurried toward the house, her mind churning. Star needed a chance to run hard, and he needed to do it soon. If her mother wouldn't let her work Star the way he needed, maybe she'd have to start training him on her own, secretly.

2

Ashleigh stared at the training schedules in front of her, but she couldn't concentrate on the paperwork. Her thoughts kept circling back to Christina and Star. She knew that Christina was upset because she wasn't letting her race Star, but she hadn't expected her daughter to say something so hurtful. Did Christina really believe that she would try to undermine Star's chances of winning the Kentucky Derby?

Ashleigh shook her head, trying to clear her thoughts. Finally she pushed the stack of papers away and leaned back, propping her feet up on the desk. Christina was totally wrong if that was what she thought. Yes, Ashleigh had had some trouble accepting Star at first, but she loved him now, just as she loved all the horses at Whitebrook. And of course she was excited to see her daughter follow in her footsteps as a winning jockey. No, she'd been telling Christina the truth about Star—after years of experience, she was certain she knew what was best for the colt as far as preparing for the Derby.

Her attention settled on a framed photo on the corner of the desk. Her mind flashed back to the day the picture had been taken. She remembered the elation and disbelief she had felt when she and Wonder had won the Classic. She had been only sixteen and an inexperienced jockey when they'd ridden in the prestigious race. Once again she felt the shock and joy at Clay Townsend's announcement that he was giving her half ownership in Wonder and her foals. She had worked so hard because she loved Wonder. She had never expected to be rewarded with such a generous gift.

Ashleigh still missed Wonder. Losing the mare had been awful. But she had gotten over that and done everything she could to help Christina and Star. It really bothered her that Christina might think she still resented Star and blamed him for Wonder's death.

She and Wonder had enjoyed a special closeness, and Ashleigh knew she would never again have that kind of bond with another horse. But, she reminded herself, she had been very lucky to have had so many great years with the mare.

She looked up at the racing pictures that covered the wall. A photo of her sitting astride Wonder's first colt, Wonder's Pride, caught her eye. She was Christina's age in the picture, already a seasoned jockey. Red-haired Samantha McLean, Ian's daughter, was standing next to the handsome chestnut racehorse, her hand on the colt's neck.

Ashleigh shook her head. Where had the years gone? Samantha was married and had a farm of her own now, and Pride was one of Whitebrook's most popular stallions.

In the photo, next to Samantha, stood a small, wiry old man with a stern expression and a battered fedora shadowing his face.

Ashleigh smiled fondly when she thought about old Charlie Burke. He had been the greatest mentor and trainer in the world. Without Charlie's help and encouragement, Wonder never would have become a winning racehorse. And after Charlie had used his years of experience to help Ashleigh become a skilled jockey, he had helped her and Samantha train Pride.

Ashleigh winced as she thought about some of the views Charlie had expressed that she hadn't agreed with until after they were proven right, almost too late to help Pride. Ashleigh still missed the old trainer, and at times she wished she could turn to him for advice again.

Her thoughts drifted back to that time in her life, and she could almost hear Charlie's voice again as they stood near Whitebrook's training track, discussing Pride's condition. How had that conversation started again? She shut her eyes and pictured the day in her mind. . . .

"I guess Clay Townsend was right," eighteen-year-old Ashleigh Griffen said, her attention on Wonder's Pride as Samantha McLean jogged the handsome chestnut colt around the training track at Whitebrook. "Pride came out of the Fountain of Youth Stakes in excellent shape. He should be able to handle the Florida Derby without any problem."

Beside her, Charlie Burke grunted.

Ashleigh glanced at the old trainer, who had his arms resting on the rail of the track, his eyes fixed on Pride. Charlie was frowning as he watched the colt work.

"He does look good," Charlie said gruffly. "But I don't want to push him. If we keep up the same workouts and schedule, he might work himself right into exhaustion or an injury." Charlie rubbed his grizzled chin thoughtfully, still watching Pride. The colt was fighting his rider, trying to pick up the pace, but Samantha was holding him back, as Charlie had instructed.

"I don't like how Mr. Townsend entered him in both the Florida race and the Blue Grass, then expects to race him in the Kentucky Derby," Charlie grumbled. "That's putting a lot of stress on the animal."

Ashleigh sighed. Charlie was right. Pride looked fantastic, but running two more strenuous races just a few weeks before the Kentucky Derby would take a lot out of any Thoroughbred, no matter how carefully planned Pride's training schedule was. In spite of their size and power, racehorses were delicate, sensitive animals that needed special care.

But as Ashleigh watched Pride fight Samantha, she couldn't help a small frown as she wondered what the answer was. The colt looked energetic and full of himself, and light jogs on the practice track didn't seem to be enough work for the high-spirited Thoroughbred. But she wasn't sure what else they could do to keep his mind fit for racing while they were trying to keep him sound and healthy.

Ashleigh cast another glance at Charlie. "He really wants to break loose out there," she commented.

"Maybe we could let him do a little breeze tomorrow, just to keep his spirits up."

Charlie shook his head. "We're going to stick with jogging and trail work," he said firmly. "Let's save the speed for the track."

One week later they shipped Pride down to Florida to prepare him for the race.

The weather at Gulfstream Park was warm, but a light breeze was blowing when Ashleigh rode Pride onto the track for the prestigious Florida Derby. Fans crowded the rails to watch the post parade. Ashleigh didn't have to look up into the grandstands to know that the Townsends, who owned a half interest in Pride, were watching the race from their comfortable seats high above the track.

Pride was in top form, prancing and bobbing his head as the pony rider guided them up the track. After a quick warm-up he loaded eagerly into the gate, snorting and stamping with impatience.

Ashleigh patted his glistening neck. "Hang on, boy," she murmured. "Just a minute and we'll be out of here."

When the starting bell clanged, Pride exploded from the gate. Ashleigh crouched over his withers, keeping a strong grip on the taut reins. The wind their speed created swept across her face, and she leaned forward. "Take it easy, Pride," she called to the galloping colt. Pride flicked his ears back, listening to her, but pressed his nose forward, fighting her grip as they thundered along the backstretch. Ashleigh darted a quick glance under her arm. The closest horses were a full length behind them.

As they pounded into the first turn, Pride refused to let up his pace, running strongly. Ashleigh checked the rest of the field, surprised to see the nearest horse several lengths behind them. "Ease up, Pride," she called to the colt, but Pride was intent on running his fastest, and it was all Ashleigh could do to keep him in check.

When they came out of the turn and headed for the finish line, she finally gave the colt his head, not sure that Pride had any more speed to give. But to her amazement, Pride gave it his all, stretching his long legs far in front of him. "We're going to do it!" she yelled. "You've got it, boy! You're going to win by a mile!"

As they charged across the finish line, Ashleigh whooped in elation. Then she focused on slowing Pride, who acted as though he could run another lap at the same pace. As she turned him back toward the winner's circle, she could see Charlie at the rail, his tattered hat crushed into a wad of felt in his hands. A broad grin stretched across the veteran trainer's face.

"Maybe we can buy Charlie a new hat with some of our winnings," she told Pride with a chuckle.

Charlie hurried out to the track to meet them, but when he got closer to Pride, his expression darkened. Hank, one of the Townsend Acres grooms, caught Pride's bridle, holding the antsy colt as Ashleigh hopped off his back. Ashleigh looked at Pride, who continued to prance, even though his chest was soaked with sweat and his sides heaved with every breath.

"That took a lot out of him," Charlie said, frowning at the agitated horse. "You should have held him back a little, Ashleigh."

"I tried," Ashleigh said quickly. "He just wanted to run like the wind."

Charlie shrugged. "Let's get that business in the winner's circle over so we can get him to the backside and take care of him."

Ashleigh smiled to herself as she stepped inside the enclosure. Leave it to Charlie to refer to the exciting moments in the circle as "that business." But she understood his concern for the horse. She felt the same way. Pride needed to get to the backside and cool down.

Clay Townsend met them in the winner's circle, smiling broadly. "Five lengths," he exclaimed, clapping his hand onto Ashleigh's shoulder. "Pride won by five lengths! The reporters are having a field day with this race. Pride will be in the headlines of all the papers tomorrow morning!"

Brad Townsend, Clay's son, stood nearby, a slim, well-dressed blond girl at his side. She looked down her nose at Ashleigh, then turned to Brad and murmured something that made him glance toward Ashleigh and laugh.

"That's Brad's new girlfriend, Lavinia Hotchkins-Ross," Hank muttered to Ashleigh. "She's a perfect match for Brad. Her family has lots of money, and she thinks she's some kind of royalty."

Ashleigh ignored Brad and Lavinia, turning to step onto the scale to have her weight checked before she hopped back onto Pride for the photo session.

Clay stood beside the chestnut colt, looking as pleased as if he had run the race himself, and Brad and Lavinia crowded in beside him, smiling for the photographer.

"I'll bet he has no problem at all running in the Blue Grass," Clay said to Charlie as they prepared to take Pride to the backside. "Then on to the Kentucky Derby and certain fame."

"I don't know," Charlie replied. "He's still wired from the race, but it wore him out. I'd like to give him a little more rest before we run him again. Maybe we should skip the Blue Grass."

Clay shook his head, then smiled for a photographer from one of the newspapers. As soon as the photo was snapped, he turned to Charlie. "But he's still got a lot of energy," Clay said.

"That's right," Brad interjected. "I'm sure he'll have plenty left for the Blue Grass, then the Derby." He looked at his father. "Townsend Acres will be a household name after this colt wins the Triple Crown."

Ashleigh watched Charlie clamp his mouth shut and turn away from Brad.

Clay gazed at Brad and nodded thoughtfully. "After that magnificent race today, he'll be the horse everyone is watching," Clay said. "And Townsend Acres can certainly use the publicity."

After the brief ceremony at the winner's circle, Ashleigh hurried off to the jockeys' lounge to change, leaving Charlie and Clay to handle the reporters while Hank led Pride to the veterinarian's barn. By the time she got to the barn, where Charlie and Hank were waiting for the drug tests required of all first- and second-place horses, Hank was walking Pride out while Charlie looked on, frowning in concern.

Pride's head drooped a little as Hank led him around, but Ashleigh wasn't too worried. "I think he'll be fine," she said to Charlie. "I'll bet that within a couple of days he'll be ready to get back on the track."

But Charlie shook his head. "I don't think running him in three tough races just before the Kentucky Derby is doing him any favors," the trainer grumbled. "I'm afraid Clay Townsend is letting Brad influence him, and he's putting the big winnings Pride is bringing in ahead of the colt's well-being."

Ashleigh frowned. After feeling how strong Pride had been that day, she thought Clay might be right. Pride could handle the races. Maybe Charlie was being a little too cautious. She didn't want to spoil the talented colt's chances for Triple Crown glory by holding him back.

By the time they returned to Lexington, Pride seemed fit and ready to run again. Samantha lavished attention on him, and Charlie insisted they keep his workouts light, much to Pride's frustration.

Ashleigh felt sorry for the powerful horse, who fought Samantha on the practice track every time he went out for his works. But Charlie was adamant. No strenuous works, nothing but light conditioning. Ashleigh didn't argue. And when the Blue Grass was run, Pride swept the field.

"The reporters are calling him the next Triple Crown champion," Ashleigh told Charlie, holding up a copy of the *Lexington Herald* the day after the race.

Charlie snorted. "We'll see," Charlie said. "I'll give him credit for how well he's run these last few races, but look at him, Ashleigh." He gestured at the colt as Samantha led him from his stall to a small paddock. "He's losing weight," the trainer commented. "The stress of the last several weeks is catching up with him."

"I think he looks good," Ashleigh said. "His weight isn't down too much. He'll gain it back before Derby day." She watched the colt dancing at the end of his lead line. "Even after yesterday, he's still very eager to run."

"He's overwrought," Charlie said, shaking his head. "We need to give him a lot of rest before the Derby. I wish we had a couple of weeks longer to let him recover."

Ashleigh knew the grueling schedule was taking its toll on the colt, but he was still in excellent shape. And he had three weeks to rest up for the Derby. She was confident he'd handle the field at Churchill Downs with the same energy he'd shown in the Fountain of Youth, the Florida Derby, and the Blue Grass.

"Hey there."

Ashleigh looked away from the photos on the wall

to see Ian McLean standing in the office doorway. The trainer's red hair was flecked with gray, but to Ashleigh, he didn't look any older than he had when Charlie, Samantha, and she were training Pride.

"Hi," she said, putting her feet down and sitting straight in her chair.

"It's getting late," Ian said. "I saw the lights on in here and thought I'd better check it out."

"I was going to review the training schedules," Ashleigh replied.

Ian raised his eyebrows. "You looked like you were in awfully deep thought for revising schedules," he commented, stepping inside the office.

"I got sidetracked," Ashleigh admitted. "I was just reliving a few memories of Pride's races."

Ian nodded, smiling fondly. "Pride," he said, affection plain in his voice. "He had a pretty amazing career on the track."

Ashleigh nodded. "I'm trying to figure out how to reassure Christina that our training schedule for Star will be as effective as the one Charlie was forced to set up for Pride. Star isn't being raced nearly as intensely as Pride was, so he should be in much better condition to run the Triple Crown series."

Ian nodded in understanding. "It isn't easy when the jockey and owner are your own daughter."

"I know," Ashleigh said. "But I hope she'll trust my judgment on this."

"I'm sure she will," Ian said. "She's just tense and excited about the Derby. I think everyone around here is a little on edge about the race."

"You're probably right," Ashleigh said, shaking her head. "I guess I'd better get up to the house for dinner."

"Me too," Ian said, grinning. "Beth is trying a new casserole tonight, and I don't want to miss out. I'll see you in the morning." Ian headed out the door as Ashleigh rose from her chair.

Charlie had kept trying to get her to slow down and pay attention to Pride's condition, but she had been so sure of the colt's stamina and heart that she hadn't listened the way she should have. She had let Clay and the excitement of the races and the competition distract her. She hoped that she and Christina wouldn't spend the next several weeks butting heads over Star's conditioning program.

She pulled her jacket on and shut off the office lights, then headed for the house, still trying to figure out how to get Christina to relax a little and not push Star the way they had pushed Pride.

3

"You're here early," Dani commented when Christina came into the barn the next morning. "Your mom hasn't even shown up yet."

Christina nodded. "I want to get Star's workout taken care of," she said, reluctant to tell the groom the real reason she had come down to the barn during the predawn hour. She really wanted to work Star the way he needed to be exercised, and she couldn't gallop him when Ashleigh was there.

"Do you want some help getting him ready?" Dani offered.

Christina quickly shook her head. "Thanks, but I'm sure you have plenty to do," she said.

Dani nodded. "Okay. I'll go put the other horses

33

out and start cleaning stalls. If you need me, just holler, okay?"

"I will," Christina reassured her, then hurried to the tack room for her grooming tools and saddle.

"We're going to do the kind of work you like today," she told Star as she fastened the girth on his saddle. "Won't it feel good to stretch your legs? Maybe then you'll settle down and start eating." Star bobbed his head, and Christina nodded. "I knew you'd agree with me, even if Mom doesn't."

It was still dark when she led Star from the barn. She didn't see any sign of her mother, and none of the house lights was on. She took a deep breath and swung onto the saddle. "Let's do this, boy," she said, guiding Star onto the track.

Despite her effort to stay relaxed, she could feel the colt picking up on her tension. She hated going behind Ashleigh's back, but she knew her mother would never let her give Star a serious workout. The night before, she and her mom had made up at dinner, and Christina knew it wasn't true that Ashleigh was trying to hold Star back because she still resented him. She felt bad she'd said that to her mother, but she'd been so upset and couldn't understand why Ashleigh wouldn't just trust her to know what was best for Star. But Ashleigh seemed so certain that babying Star was the only way to keep him strong for the upcoming Triple Crown races. Christina knew, though, that giving Star a hard workout would help keep him on his toes.

She could feel the energy coursing through Star's muscles as she jogged him along the rail. It took everything she had to keep his pace slow as they warmed up. The colt trembled with excitement as they circled the track, and finally she loosened her grip on the reins. Star took off with a burst of speed that nearly unseated Christina.

"Hold on, boy!" she exclaimed, increasing the pressure on the reins. Star fought her, keeping his fast pace as they circled the track. Christina gritted her teeth and pulled harder, awed by the incredible power of the running horse. *Mom should see Star right now*, she thought as they galloped around the track. He didn't need to be protected; he needed to race.

It was starting to get light when they came around the track a second time, and Christina noticed a figure standing near the rail. As they got closer she saw Ashleigh watching them, a deep frown on her face. Before she could slow Star, they shot by her mother. Christina groaned to herself. Now she was going to get the lecture of the century. Star fought her as she slowed him, still eager to keep up the fast pace.

"Time to face the music," she muttered to the colt as she slowed him to a jog. They rode around the practice track at the slower pace before she headed him for the gap in the rail. As they approached Ashleigh, Star tossed his head, blowing excitedly.

Christina patted his neck. "I know you liked that," she murmured. "We should be doing more gallops." Then she saw the grim look her mother was giving them, and she sighed. "But right now we're both in big trouble."

Christina dismounted and held Star, facing her mother defiantly.

"What was that about?" Ashleigh asked.

Christina stood tall. "He needed to run," she said flatly.

"I thought we worked this out last night. He needs to save what he has for the races," Ashleigh said. "Letting him run his heart out for the fun of it isn't going to do him a bit of good. We made that mistake with Pride. You know that, Chris. You've heard us talk about all those races he was forced to run."

Christina pinched her mouth shut and glared at her mother. "Star isn't Pride," she said fiercely. "Just because you almost raced Pride to death doesn't mean I want to do the same with Star."

As soon as the words were out, Christina felt a wave of guilt. Why did she keep saying such cruel things to her mother? *Because she's not listening to me*, a voice in her head responded. She knew she should apologize, but she was too upset.

"Cool him out and put him up," Ashleigh said briefly, then turned to walk into the barn.

Christina turned her attention to Star. "You needed that run," she muttered, pulling his saddle off. "She doesn't understand you like I do, Star." After Christina had walked Star out and brushed him until his coat glistened, she fed the colt and went up to the house.

When she walked into the kitchen, her father was at the stove, scrambling eggs. Mike glanced over his shoulder and raised his eyebrows. "I hear you and Star had a nice little workout," he said in a mild voice.

"He needs more work than the easy stuff Mom wants him to do," Christina said as she poured a glass of juice. She knew she sounded defensive, but her mother really was being unreasonable.

"Do you want some breakfast?" Mike asked, holding out a plate of toast and eggs.

Christina shook her head, sipping the cold juice. "I'm not hungry," she said, thinking about the expression on her mother's face when she had ridden Star off the track. Why couldn't Ashleigh see things her way? Did she think Christina was irresponsible enough to risk Star's health?

"You need to eat," Mike said, sitting down at the

table with his food. "You're going to waste away to nothing."

"Right, Dad," Christina said, draining her glass. "I eat plenty. I need to watch it so I don't put on any weight before the Derby."

Christina, at a little over five foot five, was taller than most jockeys, but with her small frame, weight wasn't a problem. Some of the jockeys she knew took extreme measures to keep their weight down and complained of being hungry all the time. But Christina could usually eat what she wanted and not worry about the calories.

"You're really worried about Star and your mom's training plan, aren't you?" Mike asked.

Christina nodded silently.

"Don't be," Mike said, giving her a reassuring smile. "Your mom knows what she's doing." He took a bite of egg and chewed thoughtfully. "She's been training winners for years."

But not my Star, Christina protested to herself. *No one understands Star the way I do.* "I know," she said aloud. "Mom's a great trainer. I'm just afraid keeping him so low-key is going to ruin his spirit. He was so excited to run in California. After being on stall rest and out to pasture for so many months, he needs to do more."

At a sound behind her, Christina snapped her

head around to see Ashleigh standing in the kitchen doorway.

Ashleigh gazed at her for a moment, then gave her a tight smile. "Maybe it isn't Star who needs to be on the track," she said.

"I want to race, too," Christina admitted. "But I'm mostly concerned about my horse."

"I understand," Ashleigh said. She poured herself a cup of coffee and sat down at the table. "I admire and respect your dedication to him, Chris. But I'm not trying to spoil Star's chances in the Derby. I want to see him win as much as you do."

The phone rang, and Christina jumped up to answer it.

"Oh—hi, Chris." Melanie Griffen's voice rang through the receiver. Christina envisioned her petite cousin sitting in a motel room in Florida, running her fingers through her short blond hair.

"Hi," Christina said. "I saw the article in the *Daily Racing Form* about Image's race. Congratulations! But they didn't say why Image didn't run in the Bonnie Miss. What made you decide to run her in the Florida Derby instead?"

The field at the Florida Derby, run at Gulfstream Park in Florida, normally consisted of the top colts in the country, while the Bonnie Miss was considered the fillies' counterpart race. But Image, the unruly filly that Melanie had helped train during the past winter, had run well against a group of strong colts, coming in second.

Melanie sighed. "Dad sort of changed plans for us."

"You switched races because of your dad?" Christina said, surprised. Will Graham, a music promoter, made a point of staying out of the training and racing end of the horse business. He had bought a half interest in Image for Melanie's sake, leaving it up to her to train and care for the willful filly.

"Yup. He's having a little financial pressure with his business, and he hoped she'd win a larger purse."

"Oh." Even though Melanie couldn't see her, Christina nodded in understanding.

"The second-place purse wasn't enough," Melanie continued. "So we sold our interest in Image."

Christina frowned, confused. The news was terrible, but Melanie didn't sound too upset. In fact, she sounded a little pleased.

"You're not telling me everything," she accused her cousin.

"Jazz bought our half of Image," Melanie said happily. "So now he's sole owner."

Jazz Taylor, a young rock star, had shared in the Grahams' purchase of Image earlier in the year. It had taken Melanie some time to see beyond the musician's public image, but she had eventually realized that Jazz was as much an animal lover as she was, and they'd ended up becoming close friends.

"He's giving me full control of training and racing her," Melanie said. "And guess what?" Before Christina could ask, Melanie continued. "We've decided to enter Image in the Kentucky Derby. Isn't that great?"

Christina felt her jaw drop. Image was going to run in the Derby? "Yeah, it's . . . great, Mel," she said, forcing enthusiasm into her voice.

She and Melanie hadn't been on the track together since the previous month. During a race at Keeneland, Melanie had accused Christina of bumping her horse into Image. The stewards upheld the race standings, but Christina couldn't stop feeling as though her win had been clouded by the accusation. Melanie had apologized later, but still, things weren't completely back to normal between them. In fact, Christina wondered if Melanie had sounded a little surprised when she answered the phone. Had Mel been hoping to get one of Christina's parents instead?

No, she was probably just being silly. Even so, she wasn't sure how she felt about racing against her cousin in the Kentucky Derby. *Well*, she decided, *all Star and I can do is run our best.*

"Joe and I will be home in a few days," Melanie

continued. Joe Kisner, one of Whitebrook's full-time grooms, had driven Melanie and Image to the Gulfstream track for their race. "Image is resting up, and Joe is bracing himself for the drive home. She was horrible on the way down here. Now that she's run a great race, maybe Image will be nice and ladylike for the trip home."

"Good luck," Christina said dryly. Image definitely had a big attitude, but Melanie always rose to the occasion and managed to handle the stubborn, high-spirited filly.

"See you soon," Melanie said. "Tell your parents I said hi."

Christina hung up, then wandered back to the kitchen, slightly dazed over the news about Image.

She thought over the other horses entering the Derby that she already knew about. Gratis, owned by Ben al-Rihani's Tall Oaks Farm, shared some bloodlines with Ashleigh's Wonder. Christina had ridden the difficult colt in a few races, and she knew he was going to be a serious threat on the track. He was being trained by Cindy McLean, Ian's daughter. Then there was Celtic Mist. Christina didn't have the same personal experience with the Townsend Acres horse, but she knew Celtic Mist could be a threat. But now Image would be making the competition that much tougher.

Christina shook her head, trying not to think about the increasingly intimidating challengers. She needed to concentrate on getting Star ready, not waste her energy fretting about the other horses and jockeys.

"What's up?" her father asked, noticing her concerned expression.

"Melanie is going to race Image in the Derby," Christina announced.

"That's exciting news," Mike said, carrying his plate to the sink. "And not surprising at all. Image definitely has the speed and the heart to compete."

"Three horses with ties to Whitebrook in the Kentucky Derby," Ashleigh commented. "What a race that's going to be."

Mike nodded thoughtfully. "No matter how things go, this will be great publicity for the farm."

Ashleigh looked from Mike to Christina, then smiled. "Your father and I were talking while you were on the phone."

"About what?" Christina asked, still thinking about Melanie and Image. She was happy for her cousin, but she still couldn't shake the memory of Melanie protesting their last race together. She sighed and hoped they were past that.

"You keep saying Star needs to get out and run," Ashleigh said.

"Yes," Christina said emphatically, hope springing to life again. "He really does, Mom."

Ashleigh nodded. "I wonder if maybe *you* want to be on the track so much that you're projecting your feelings onto Star."

Christina started to protest, but Ashleigh shook her head, and Christina fell silent.

"I entered Raven in a race at Turfway this weekend. Why don't you ride her? Maybe you can get named in a few other races, too. It might take your mind off the Derby stress."

Christina shrugged. "Sure," she said. Racing at Turfway sounded like fun. But it was too bad there wasn't a race they could enter Star in. She knew she wasn't just saying Star wanted to race because it was what she wanted to do. He needed the challenge to keep on his toes, but as long as her mother refused to see that, it was never going to happen.

4

Raven stood in the aisle in front of her stall at the Turf-way track, her ears pricked. Dani finished wrapping her legs while Christina ran a comb through her shiny black tail.

"I'd better change into my silks," Christina said, glancing at her watch. "It's getting close to post time." She left Dani to finish preparing Raven for their race and headed for the jockeys' lounge.

In the locker room Christina pulled on her blue-and-white Whitebrook silks and weighed in with the clerk of scales. In a few minutes she was at the viewing paddock with Mike and Ashleigh, waiting for Dani to bring Raven out from the saddling area near the pad-dock.

"Watch out for the number three horse," Ashleigh said, nodding toward a high-strung gray filly that fought its handler as the horses entered the paddock. The filly reared and lashed out, baring its teeth as the woman leading it struggled to keep the fiery horse under control.

"I will," Christina promised, then turned her attention to Raven as Dani brought the filly around the paddock. The Whitebrook filly's black coat glistened in the April sunlight. Her neck was arched, and she pranced in place when Dani stopped her in front of them.

"Good luck out there," Mike said, giving Christina a boost onto the filly's back.

"Have a great ride," Ashleigh said.

"We will," Christina responded, buckling her chin strap and jabbing her toes into the stirrups as Dani led Raven to the waiting pony horse. Christina wasn't worried about the race. Raven was in great form, the track conditions were perfect, and she was eager to put the filly through her paces. Her only regret was that she wasn't riding Star onto the track. Riding Raven was exciting, but it didn't do anything to help Star.

She patted Raven's neck as the pony rider led them onto the track. "We're going to do great, aren't we, girl?" she murmured, posting to Raven's lilting trot.

After a quick warm-up gallop, they loaded into the starting gate and waited for the bell. It seemed to take forever before one of the gate crew called, "One back," and the last horse was loaded. Christina tangled her fingers into Raven's silky mane and leaned forward, prepared for the explosive start of the race.

After a tense pause, the bell sounded and the gate snapped open. Raven burst onto the track with the rest of the fillies, and Christina angled her toward the rail. A big bay filly crowded close to Raven, pushing them against the rail. Christina gritted her teeth and glared at the bay's rider.

"Sorry," the other jockey yelled, dragging at his mount's right rein to keep from bumping into Raven.

Christina hunkered over Raven's withers, guiding the galloping horse away from the rail, determined to put more distance between them and the other Thoroughbreds. Raven felt strong and steady under her, and Christina's confidence blossomed as they held the lead.

"You're doing great," she told Raven. The filly stretched her neck and pushed the pace, while Christina kept a firm grip on the reins, trying to rate Raven as they flew past the poles marking the furlongs.

This is the way the Kentucky Derby should go, she thought. She and Star would be in the lead, taking the field by surprise, and they would win by several lengths, with no other horse even close to them.

As they tore down the backstretch, Christina

glanced under her arm, startled to see the number three horse charging up, shooting past the big bay and a powerful-looking chestnut filly. It looked to Christina as though the gray was gaining on them with every stride.

You'd better quit daydreaming, she scolded herself, turning her attention back to the view from between Raven's ears. She leaned forward, urging the filly to speed up.

"Give it a little more, girl," she called, easing her grip on the reins a bit as they came out of the turn. But in spite of Raven's efforts, the gray blew past them. Raven flattened her ears against her head.

"Let's go!" Christina shouted at Raven as the gray sped by. *I should have been paying attention,* Christina berated herself.

She leaned forward on Raven's shoulders, balancing lightly on the stirrups as they galloped toward the finish line. Raven willingly poured on more power, but the bay filly seemed to have the same idea, moving up beside them and running strongly. The three racehorses charged up the track, the gray in the lead, with Raven and the bay neck and neck for second place.

The gray's jockey headed his mount toward the rail, but Christina could see enough of a gap between the filly and the inside to slip past them if Raven would just take her speed up another notch.

Christina pushed her fisted hands against Raven's pumping neck, and Raven responded willingly, her breath coming in deep whooshes as she stretched out. Foamy sweat streaked the black filly's shoulders as she caught up with the gray. At Christina's urging, Raven dove forward into the tiny gap between the other horse and the rail.

Suddenly Christina realized with horror that the space wasn't wide enough for Raven to slide into. She frantically tried to slow the galloping horse, her heart thumping like crazy, but it was too late. Raven brushed the inside rail and bounced into the gray's side.

The wreck seemed to happen in slow motion. Christina felt Raven falter as the gray responded to the bump with an energetic buck, knocking Raven back toward the rail. Then Raven was going down and Christina was airborne. Beside her she saw the gray's front legs buckling and the jockey flipping over the filly's shoulder.

Then her only thoughts were of Raven, hoping fervently that the black filly was all right. She landed abruptly, the hard contact with the track knocking the breath out of her. She felt herself skidding and rolling on the ground as the rest of the horses thundered by, heading to the finish line. Even after they passed, the pounding of their hooves rang in her ears.

She lay still for a moment, trying to catch her

breath. A quick assessment reassured her that nothing had been broken, and she pushed herself to her knees as a track car stopped nearby. Several members of the crew leaped from the vehicle and raced to the scene. A medic caught Christina by the elbow as she scrambled to her feet.

"You shouldn't move until we check you over," he said firmly, but Christina shook her head, fumbling with her helmet's chin strap as she looked back to check on Raven. She saw the gray filly staggering to her feet. The filly's jockey was standing by the horse, holding her reins. He petted the stunned animal as more members of the track crew hurried over to them.

Near the rail, she saw Raven lying motionless on the track.

"No!" Christina cried. She pulled away from the medic to run to the stricken filly's side. Christina dropped to her knees and pressed her hand to Raven's neck. Raven groaned softly, and Christina felt tears well up in her eyes. "You need to get up," she said desperately as hands caught her from behind and pulled her away.

"No!" she cried again, trying to wrench free. "Raven," she called, then suddenly she was enveloped in her father's arms. She collapsed against him, unable to control her sobs.

Christina let her father guide her to the outside edge of the track, away from all the activity. Ashleigh put her arms around Christina while Mike hurried back to check on Raven. In a moment he returned.

"The crew got her up," he said.

"Is she okay?" Christina asked, feeling the sick knot in her stomach ease a little. She tried to look toward the commotion on the track, but Mike blocked her view. The relief Christina felt was short-lived when she caught sight of her father's bleak expression.

"They loaded her onto the van," Mike said. "We need to get over to the veterinarian's barn. It doesn't look good."

The knot in her stomach tightened again, and Christina was afraid she was going to be sick right in front of the grandstand. Numbly she let her parents lead her toward the backside, feeling as though she had been plunged into a nightmare.

By the time they reached the barn, two handlers were putting Raven into a narrow stall. Christina's heart sank as she saw the filly hop on three legs from the back of the van into the stall. Her saddle had been pulled off, and drying sweat streaked her sides.

Beside Christina, Ashleigh let out a soft, pained murmur. Christina bit back a fresh flood of tears, watching in dismay as the handlers strapped a sling under Raven's belly so that she could keep the weight off her leg. A gray-haired man wearing a badge identifying himself as Sam Reeves, DVM, stepped into the stall and began examining the injured Thoroughbred.

After a few minutes he glanced up at the Reeses, a deep frown creasing his forehead. "I'm sure she's torn some tendons," he said. "We'll do X rays to check for any broken bones."

An assistant stopped at the stall with a cart loaded with medical equipment. Christina took a step toward Raven, but her father pulled her back. "Let them work, Chris," he said quietly, keeping his arm around her shoulders.

Christina watched in silence as the vet took X rays of Raven's shoulders and front legs, then finished his examination of the injured filly.

Christina closed her eyes as the vet strode away with the metal containers of X-ray film. *Let her be okay*, she said to herself. *Just let Raven be okay.*

She stood by the filly's stall, stroking Raven's dark nose while they waited for the vet to return. "I'm sorry, girl," she murmured, running her hand along Raven's glossy cheek. The filly nudged at her hand, and Christina swallowed around a hard lump in her throat. "You're going to be all right," she said, wishing she knew she was telling Raven the truth.

When the gray-haired vet returned, his expression was gloomy. He looked at Mike and Ashleigh and shook his head. "There aren't any broken bones," he said.

But that's good news, Christina told herself. *Why is he looking so serious?*

"However," he continued, "it does appear that she has completely torn the tendons and ligaments in her right leg. I'd recommend euthanasia."

"No!" The word came out before Christina could stop herself. "We can't put Raven down." She turned to her parents, panic welling up inside her. "Don't let them." She stood in front of the stall as though she could protect Raven from the vet's bleak words.

Ashleigh glanced at Mike, then sighed. "Is there anything we can do before we make that kind of decision?" she asked Dr. Reeves.

The vet shrugged. "There's a possibility we could reattach the tendons," he said. "But there are no guarantees she'll even be able to walk after that. I don't know if you want to put her through surgery. The odds aren't very good. Even if she does pull through, she'll never be sound again."

Mike nodded. "I'd like to have our vet come in to discuss her condition with you," he said. He left to call Dr. Seymour, Whitebrook's regular vet, while Ashleigh and Christina watched Dr. Reeves give Raven an injection for pain. In a minute the filly's eyes glazed over and she began dozing.

Christina stood motionless in front of the stall until Ashleigh gave her shoulder a squeeze. "You need to get out of your silks," Ashleigh said. "I'll stay with Raven."

Christina moved like a robot through the backside to the jockeys' lounge. Several riders looked up as she came through the door, but no one said anything to her. Christina hurried into the women's locker room. She sank onto one of the benches, burying her face in her hands. Tears burned hot behind her eyes, but before she could give in to them, she heard the door open and two jockeys walked into the locker room, talking about the races they had just finished. They both looked in her direction and fell silent. Christina jumped to her feet and turned away, quickly peeling off her silks. Without bothering to shower, she pulled on her jeans and T-shirt.

When she returned to the vet's barn, Mike and Ashleigh were standing with Dr. Seymour and Dr. Reeves, looking at Raven.

Dr. Seymour nodded to Christina, then turned back to Mike and Ashleigh. "I agree with Dr. Reeves," he said. "Your options are limited. We can try surgery, but she may not be able to walk again. Which means she won't even be useful as a broodmare."

"We have to try," Ashleigh said.

Christina sighed with relief. At least they were going to give Raven a chance.

"We'll do everything we can," Dr. Seymour said.

The vets walked away, and Christina looked from her mother to her father, hoping to see some sign that they believed Raven would pull through. But they both wore the same grim frown, and Christina could see tears in her mother's eyes. Then a new thought struck her, and she felt a fresh wave of sickness come over her. "Melanie," she breathed. Her cousin was crazy about Raven. What would she say when she heard what Christina had done to the horse? "She's going to be so upset," Christina said. "How am I going to tell her about Raven?"

"I'll handle it," Ashleigh said.

Christina knew she should be the one to talk to Melanie, but she didn't know if she could face her cousin, and she nodded. "Thanks, Mom," she said, then added, "But this was all my fault. I made a stupid move, and Raven is paying the price. I'll take care of all of her vet bills."

When neither of her parents responded, Christina swallowed hard. They agreed. She had ridden carelessly and caused a terrible accident.

A man walked into the barn and strode toward them. Christina recognized him as one of the trainers who regularly had horses at Turfway. He glared at Christina.

"I'm having a meeting with the track officials about you," he said. "You could have gotten someone killed, riding like that. If you can't pay attention, you shouldn't be on the track." He spun around and stormed off, shaking his head and muttering under his breath.

Christina stared at his back. She hadn't thought she could feel any more down, but she realized that she agreed with the trainer. She had been careless, thinking about Star and the Derby instead of focusing on the race.

"Don't worry about him," Mike said to Christina. "He has a reputation for being a hothead."

"I deserve it," Christina said miserably. "I wasn't paying attention, and I crowded his horse."

Ashleigh gazed at her. "We'll just have to see what the officials say when they review the video," she said calmly. After making sure that Raven was comfortable and being well cared for, the Reeses left Turfway, driving home in gloomy silence.

Christina sat by the phone all afternoon, waiting for a call from the track stewards. But when the phone finally rang, she couldn't bring herself to answer it. Instead, Ashleigh took the call.

Christina sat on the edge of a chair in the living

room, her hands clenched between her knees, waiting tensely to hear the outcome of the stewards' meeting. She could hear her mother, but Ashleigh's end of the conversation consisted mostly of "uh-huh" and "okay." Finally the call ended.

This is it, Christina thought when Ashleigh came into the living room. *I'm going to be suspended from racing. There won't be a Derby for Star and me. But maybe that's not such a bad thing. It could have been Star on the track this morning.* The thought turned her body to ice. She couldn't even imagine what she'd be feeling right now if that had been the case.

But Ashleigh didn't seem upset when Christina looked up at her. "The stewards agreed that although you were close, the other horse contributed to the accident by crowding Raven into the rail," Ashleigh told her. "There won't be any disciplinary action."

A rush of relief surged through Christina, but it was mixed with lingering terror over the idea that Star could have been the horse she'd badly injured. She shuddered at the thought of waiting to hear if Star would live or die.

That night she spent the evening in Star's stall, trying to lavish attention on him. But the wreck kept replaying in her mind. "What am I going to do, Star?" she asked the colt, working a brush along his flank. "I don't think I could stand it if something happened to you in a race. I'd never forgive myself."

Star shoved his nose at her, demanding to have his ears rubbed. Christina obliged, absently massaging his poll. But her thoughts drifted to Raven and how upset Melanie was going to be when she found out what had happened. Star butted her with his head, and Christina realized she had stopped petting the demanding colt. "Sorry," she said, forcing herself to pay more attention to grooming Star.

When she went to bed later, her sleep was filled with a continuous nightmare as she relived the accident over and over.

Christina's alarm went off early the next morning, and she started to sit up, but fell back with a groan. She lay still for a moment, trying to figure out if there was a part of her that didn't hurt. Finally she sat up slowly, convinced that every inch of her body had to be covered in bruises. There was no way she could climb onto a horse's back that day. On top of her aches and pains, visions of Raven cartwheeling onto the track still filled her head. She kept flashing to an image of Star falling the way Raven had, and she felt sick. She just wanted to soak in a warm bath, crawl back into bed, and not risk putting her precious colt through what Raven was suffering.

"Chris!" she heard her mother call from downstairs. "I'll be down at the barn. Dani is getting Star ready for you to work. Hurry up."

Christina walked slowly down the stairs and into the kitchen. "I'm not going to work Star," she told her mother.

Ashleigh stopped pouring the coffee into her lidded mug and turned slowly to face Christina, her face set in determined lines. "You are not going to let yesterday stop you from riding," she said.

"My carelessness may have killed Raven," Christina said tersely. "What makes you think I'd be any better with Star?"

"Yesterday was an accident," Ashleigh replied, her voice softening. "You still need to keep Star in shape for the Derby."

Christina felt her shoulders sag. She shook her head. "I don't know about racing Star in the Derby," she said.

"Chris," Ashleigh said, setting the cup on the counter. She crossed the room and rested her hands on Christina's shoulders, looking into her eyes. "You will be fine. We'll do everything we can for Raven, but don't cheat Star out of his chance to race in the Derby. It's important for you and for him, and for Whitebrook, too." Ashleigh headed for the door. "Get

59

upstairs and change," she said, pausing before she pulled the door shut behind her. "Star's waiting for you." Then she was gone.

Christina thought about going back to bed, but instead she took a hot shower, letting the water ease her sore muscles, then pulled on jeans and a sweatshirt. By the time she walked down to the barn, she was feeling a little more limber, but she groaned with pain as she swung onto Star's back.

Dani gave her a worried look. "Are you all right?" she asked quietly.

Christina gritted her teeth and nodded. "I'll survive," she muttered, guiding Star onto the track. After a few minutes of warming up, she felt herself relax on the colt, slipping into the familiar rhythm of Star's movements. She patted his neck. "We'll be fine," she said to him, trying to sound confident. "We're going to be just great on the track, aren't we?" Star flicked his ears back, listening to her, and she hoped he believed her—because she wasn't sure she believed it herself.

5

"That's my girl," Ashleigh said to herself, watching Christina start Star's warm-up laps. "Don't let Raven's accident stop you." She sighed. Christina and Raven's wreck had been terrible, but unfortunately accidents like those were part of the harsh realities of racing Thoroughbreds. She hoped Christina had it in her to overcome the trauma of Raven's injury and keep racing.

Ashleigh tried to shut out her own concerns about Raven. She had plenty of experience with these situations, but it never got any easier to see one of her horses hurt. She gave her head a quick shake, then leaned against the practice track rail, keeping a close eye on the way Star moved. The colt looked good, his muscles rippling under his sleek chestnut coat. His strides were long and even, his eagerness to break into a gallop obvious with every step he took. But she still believed that letting him work hard might set him back, something she didn't want to risk. Star had struggled to overcome a lot of challenges. They couldn't afford to push him, even though Christina was adamant that the colt could handle more stress than Ashleigh would allow her to expose him to.

No, she had made her decision and she would stick to it—there wouldn't be any other races before the Derby was run. It might make Christina feel better, but Ashleigh didn't want to take any chances as far as Star was concerned. In the long run, she knew her daughter would be happier to have a Derby win than an overworked horse.

Star and Christina rounded the curve in the track at a steady jog. To Ashleigh's relief, it looked as though Christina had settled comfortably into the pace and seemed to be relaxing a little. She rode Star past Ashleigh, her attention completely focused on the colt. To Ashleigh, it appeared that Christina and Star had become one creature.

Ashleigh felt love for her daughter well up inside her—she was so proud of her. She remembered watching Pride and Samantha riding on the same track years earlier. If Christina had had flaming red hair, Ashleigh would have sworn it was Samantha and Pride she was watching jog along Whitebrook's track.

Samantha had worked hard to take care of Pride during the height of his racing career. She had seen better than anyone the toll his three-year-old season was taking on him. Ashleigh remembered arguing with Samantha about how Pride was handling the stress of being ridden in so many races during a short time. So many years had passed since Pride ran in the Kentucky Derby, but as she thought about it now, it seemed like only a short while ago. In her mind Ashleigh could see Samantha as a teenager, doing everything she could to protect Pride from the grueling schedule of races the Townsends had pressed on him. . . .

"He's worn out," Samantha said, stopping Pride at the practice track rail after his morning work. "Look at him, Ashleigh. He needs a break."

Ashleigh ran her hand along Pride's shiny red-gold neck. She had to agree with Samantha. The colt did look tired. But she shook her head. "We can't just pull him out of the Derby, Sammy," she said. "Even if we tried to, the Townsends would hire a different jockey and race him anyway. I only have half ownership in him."

Samantha hopped from the colt's back and shook her head at Ashleigh, her eyes filled with disgust. "You're going to have half ownership in a broken-down horse if we don't give him a rest."

"There isn't anything I can do," Ashleigh replied, then added, "Besides, he looked good for you today. The easy works Charlie is having you put Pride through aren't stressing him at all. I think he'll be fine for the Derby."

"It isn't just the Derby," Samantha said, pulling Pride's saddle from his back. "There'll be the Preakness and the Belmont and who knows how many more races after that."

Ashleigh slipped Pride's halter onto his head. "Let's just worry about one race at a time," she said. Pride tossed his head and snorted loudly, making Ashleigh smile. "See?" she said to Samantha. "He wants to run."

Samantha shrugged. "He isn't mine to make decisions about," she said. "If he was, I'd give him a long vacation from the track. He needs it." She rubbed the colt's neck, then planted a kiss on the end of his nose. "Come on, Pride. Let's walk you out."

Ashleigh watched Samantha lead the handsome chestnut colt away, and exhaled heavily. She knew Samantha felt very protective of the colt, but she was sure he'd make a magnificent showing in the Derby.

A week later, they moved Pride to Churchill Downs and began gearing up for the biggest race of his career. Ashleigh felt the tension around the backside build as Derby day neared. She could tell Pride sensed it, too, but Samantha spent every minute she had with the colt, helping him stay relaxed, and Pride seemed to thrive on the attention she gave him. *He'll be fine*, Ashleigh reassured herself.

On the day of the Derby the Churchill Downs grandstand was packed with fans eagerly waiting for the start of the race. Pride pranced past the crowd during the post parade, and Ashleigh, perched on the racing saddle, felt nervous excitement knotting her stomach. She searched the grandstand, finally spotting Samantha's red hair. She waved, and Samantha let go of the binoculars she had pressed to her face to wave back. Beside Samantha, Ashleigh could see Samantha's boyfriend, Tor Nelson, and Sammy's friend Yvonne. Charlie and Ian were sitting in front of them.

Ashleigh patted Pride's gleaming shoulder, pleased at how calm and alert the colt was. Some of the other horses on the track were bucking and fighting the pony riders, but Pride moved along smartly, as though he was in a hurry to get to the gate and get down to business.

Ashleigh felt her own tension fade a little. Pride was more than ready for this race. They settled into the number five gate, and Ashleigh shifted her weight forward onto Pride's shoulders, bracing herself for the start. When the gate banged open, Pride blasted from the chute like a rocket, and Ashleigh urged him toward the rail slightly ahead of the rest of the field.

Pride ran easily, but Ashleigh fought down a surge of confidence. All of the colts running were impressive racehorses. An early lead didn't mean Pride would stay in front the whole race.

She glanced under her arm and saw the number three horse, a colt named Count Abdul, moving up beside them. She groaned a little, feeling Pride tense as he sensed the other horse gaining on their position. She held the chestnut colt steady, trying to keep him from putting on a burst of speed too soon. As they shot past the pole marking the first half mile, she knew they were pushing the pace. But Count Abdul kept the pressure on, and it was all Ashleigh could do to keep Pride from exploding out from under her.

Count Abdul moved up beside Pride, and the colts ran neck and neck, moving rapidly toward the mile marker. She heard the announcer call that another colt, Ultrasound, was moving into third place.

"We can do this, boy," she called to Pride, loosening

her grip on the reins a fraction. The colt responded with a fresh surge of power, flying ahead of Count Abdul to dash across the finish line. Ashleigh glanced back in time to see Count Abdul cross the line two full lengths behind Pride.

"We did it!" she cried, slowing the colt as they galloped past the grandstand again. She could feel Pride shaking as she brought him down to a canter. She circled him back toward the rail. By the time she got him down to a trot she could see the McLeans, Tor, Yvonne, and Charlie hurrying down the grandstand steps. They met at the winner's circle, where Clay Townsend was already waiting, along with Brad and his haughty girlfriend, Lavinia.

After the photo session and a few minutes of posing for the television cameras, Ashleigh quickly dismounted, watching anxiously as Charlie and Samantha led Pride away. The colt was still breathing heavily, and his coat was streaked with sweat after the hard race. After the photo session with the Townsends, she hurried to change out of her silks, then went looking for Pride.

Samantha was walking the colt out, and she glared at Ashleigh when she saw her. "He's exhausted," Samantha said flatly. Samantha was calm and reassuring to Pride, but her face showed her frustration and concern for the colt. Ashleigh understood how Samantha felt, but there wasn't a lot she could do.

Charlie nodded in agreement. "You shouldn't have let him run so hard," he told Ashleigh.

Ashleigh bristled. "Count Abdul was pushing him," she said defensively. "I could barely hold him back."

"He needs a long rest," Samantha said when she brought Pride to a halt near Ashleigh and Charlie.

Pride's head was down, and his eyes seemed to be missing the brightness that usually shone from them.

"He ran hard today," Ashleigh said. "He'll snap back in time for the Preakness."

"You're going to ruin him," Samantha said, almost in tears, as she stroked Pride's long neck.

"I'm doing the best I can," Ashleigh said. "The Townsends won't back off his schedule, so we just have to work with it." Inside, though, she couldn't help wondering whether she had pushed Pride too hard, letting him run all out to win. He still had two races to go in the Triple Crown series. She knew Samantha and Charlie were right—Pride needed rest, not more races. But there was nothing she could do about that.

• • •

The thudding of hooves on the track brought Ashleigh back to Whitebrook and the present.

As Christina brought Star around the track again, Ashleigh watched her restrain the eager colt. She sighed sympathetically. She knew how much the pair wanted to get into another race, but they didn't understand that they needed to be patient. She wished she had been able to keep Pride from having to work so hard. Things probably could have ended differently for him that year if he hadn't been raced so heavily. She didn't want the same thing to happen to Star.

Star's racing schedule was much lighter than Pride's had been, but in light of his recent illness, Ashleigh was sure that pushing Star right now would be the worst mistake they could make in his conditioning. Christina was just going to have to trust her. But after the disastrous race the day before, Christina needed a boost to her confidence, too.

Ashleigh rubbed her chin with her thumb, watching Christina bring Star down to a walk as they neared the gap in the rail. She knew she had to think of something that would help both Christina and Star, but even though she racked her brain for a solution, nothing came to mind.

6

"I'll take care of Raven's stall myself," Christina told Dani as they stood in front of Raven's specially equipped stall. Raven's weight was supported by the sling Mike and Ian had set up. The filly stood quietly in the middle of the stall, sedated by medications the vet had provided. She would be confined until Dr. Seymour felt she had healed enough to attempt walking, which meant cleaning the bedding frequently.

"She's going to be all right," Dani reassured Christina as they looked in on the lethargic filly.

"I hope so," Christina replied, but her heart ached at the sight of Raven looking so listless and weak.

Dani tilted her head at Christina in sympathy. "I don't mind cleaning her stall," she said gently. "You need to spend more time with Star during the next few weeks, anyway."

"Thanks," Christina said. "But I owe it to Raven. It's the least I can do." She cringed inwardly. It was definitely true, but there was also something else she couldn't say to Dani. As excited as she'd been to race Star in the Derby before the accident with Raven, she had so many mixed emotions now. She still felt her heart rate speed up when she imagined herself and Star in the winner's circle of the first jewel of the Triple Crown, but the image kept being replaced by one of Star looking as weak as Raven did right now. How could she get past that fear and give Star the chance he deserved?

As she turned to leave the aisle a truck and horse trailer pulled to a stop near the open barn door. Ashleigh and Ian came out of the barn office and headed for the door as Joe climbed from the truck. Melanie sprang from the passenger's side and dashed around the front of the truck, waving excitedly to her aunt, then hurried to the back of the trailer.

Christina hesitated, knowing that her cousin's elated mood would be spoiled as soon as she heard about Raven's injuries. Melanie adored Raven, and Christina knew her cousin was going to be devastated if the filly had to be put down.

71

She heard a loud bang that she knew was Image kicking the trailer. The sound was followed by the rumbling of Image's hooves on the trailer floor, followed by a loud whinny as Melanie brought the filly out of the trailer.

From inside the barn came an answering whinny, bringing a smile to Christina's face. Pirate Treasure, a blind Thoroughbred who served as Image's companion when she was at the farm, was waiting for his pasturemate.

Image pranced into the barn, her head high and her tail flagged. "She's still wired from the race," Melanie explained to Ian and Ashleigh. "She's more than ready to run again. I can hardly wait until May. We're going to ride in the Kentucky Derby! Can you believe it?"

"That is so wonderful," Ashleigh said. "It's going to be an exciting time for all of us."

Christina slumped against Raven's stall. The tension she felt building up inside her every time she thought of the Derby was starting to make her feel a little queasy.

"We put Image in the stall next to Pirate's," Ashleigh said. "I'm sure she'll settle down quickly once she's around him again."

Ashleigh followed Melanie as she led the filly away. Christina let out a sigh. She was tempted to flee the barn and hide, but eventually she was going to have to face Melanie. Avoiding her wouldn't make the situation with Raven any easier. She left Raven's stall to stand by Star, who hung his head over the stall door and demanded attention. She rubbed the colt's soft nose while she waited for Melanie to return from the other end of the barn.

"She's going to be furious with me," Christina said morosely. Star bobbed his head as though agreeing with her. Christina gave him a sour look. "You're not making this any easier, you know," she said, running her fingers over the swirl of white on his forehead.

"No!"

Christina winced as she heard Melanie's cry from the end of the barn. Her mother must have told Melanie the awful news about Raven. Footsteps pounded in the aisle as Melanie raced through the barn, stopping abruptly at Raven's stall.

Christina watched her cousin stare at the black filly, who looked awful, cradled by the wide canvas sling.

"Oh, Raven," Melanie said tearfully. "What did Chris do to you?"

At the words, Christina went rigid.

Melanie leaned into the stall and petted the quiet filly, then turned and saw Christina standing quietly at Star's stall. Her pained expression quickly transformed into a furious glare, her eyes blazing. She strode over to Christina, and every step she took seemed to bring Christina closer to bursting into tears. "I can't believe it. How could you?" Melanie demanded, her voice trembling.

Christina struggled against the pressure behind her eyelids and gazed as steadily as she could into her cousin's eyes. "I didn't hurt Raven on purpose," she protested softly. "It was an accident, Mel."

"You never would have ridden Star into a wreck like that," Melanie said sharply.

Christina started to speak, then clamped her mouth shut. There was nothing she could say. Melanie was too angry to listen, and besides, Christina still felt she deserved full blame for Raven's injury. If she'd had her mind completely on Raven's race instead of fretting about Star and the Derby, she probably would have been able to avoid the crash.

Melanie shook her head. "Maybe you should have stuck with eventing," she said bitterly. "At least Raven would have been safe."

Christina let her breath out in a shocked whoosh of air. Melanie whirled away and stormed out of the barn.

Christina stared after her, then turned back to Star, burying her face against the colt's warm neck. "Maybe she's right," she mumbled. "I was reckless with Raven." She looked up at the colt. Star gazed at her with his soft, dark eyes. "I would never take that kind of chance with you," she said.

"It sounds like Melanie is taking this pretty hard," Ian said from behind Christina.

She turned to face the trainer, biting her lower lip and nodding. "She loves Raven so much," she said sadly. "If Raven doesn't recover, Melanie will never forgive me."

Ian raised his eyebrows. "Never is a long time, Chris. And we're doing everything we can for the filly. Don't give up hope, okay?"

Melanie managed to avoid Christina for the rest of the afternoon, and she wasn't at the table for dinner. The next morning when Christina carried her schoolbooks out to the Blazer, she saw Melanie walking down to the McLeans' cottage, where Kevin was waiting for her in Beth's car.

Christina watched the car pull out of the driveway and sighed. She wished Melanie could see how awful she felt about Raven. Melanie was taking Raven's condition even harder than Christina had expected, but she didn't know how to approach her cousin. Ian's advice to give Melanie time didn't seem to be helping, but there was nothing else Christina could do.

When she pulled up by the barn after school, there was a strange vehicle parked near the barn door. Christina walked inside, following the voices she heard to the barn office. Her mother and father stood near the office door, talking to a woman with a notepad.

Christina recognized the writer for the local paper and groaned inwardly. She didn't want to talk to any reporters just then. Even though the papers were focusing on the horses slated for the Derby, Christina was afraid the wreck with Raven would come up, and she didn't want to relive that horrible incident for a news-hungry reporter. But before she could slip past the office and on to Star's stall, the woman turned, and her eyes lit up.

"Christina!" the reporter said. "I'm so glad I caught you. I have some questions about Wonder's Star."

From behind the reporter, her father shot her an apologetic look.

Christina smiled politely at the reporter. "My parents probably answered your questions better than I could," she said, inching away.

"I want to know how you feel about your cousin and her filly, Image, running against you in the Derby," the reporter persisted, taking a step toward Christina. "It must be pretty tense for both of you."

Christina forced a smile. "Of course we're both excited about the Derby," she said. "But we've ridden against each other in plenty of races, so this won't be anything new."

"But it seems to me there must be some animosity between the two of you," the reporter pushed. "Didn't Ms. Graham protest the last race the two of you were in together?"

Christina caught her breath, trying to think of a reasonable answer.

Ashleigh stepped forward quickly, standing next to Christina. "We're all excited about the Derby," she said easily. "Both girls are very competitive, but they're also very close. They'll both ride well at Churchill Downs in May, and of course the fastest horse on the track will win."

After a few more questions directed at Ashleigh and Mike, the reporter left. Christina heaved a sigh of relief. "As soon as I see Star, I'm going to change and get Raven's stall cleaned," she said.

Ashleigh shook her head. "Melanie already did that," she replied.

Christina felt her stomach drop. Melanie didn't even want Christina to muck out Raven's stall? Was her cousin ever going to get over being upset with her?

The next morning when Christina rode onto the

practice track, she spotted Melanie on Image. Ashleigh stood at Melanie's knee, talking to her. Christina paused Star by the gap in the rail.

In a moment Ashleigh glanced up. When she saw Christina, she waved to her. "Come here," she called.

Christina walked Star onto the track and jogged him toward her mother and cousin. But as she got closer, Melanie turned Image and rode away, circling the track.

"Don't be too upset," Ashleigh comforted Christina. "Melanie is very worried about Raven, and she's on edge about the Derby. She isn't handling the stress too well, either, Chris."

Christina gripped Star's reins, fighting down her hurt feelings. "Doesn't she know I would never have hurt Raven on purpose?" she asked.

Ashleigh sighed. "You'll just have to give her some time, Chris."

Great—her mother was telling her exactly what Ian had already said. But how much time would it take for Melanie to forgive her?

"What was it you wanted to tell me?" Christina asked, trying to concentrate on how she was working with Star. Whether or not Melanie got over being mad at her, Star needed his workout. Her mixed feelings about the Derby weren't helping the colt at all.

"Do a mile at an easy jog," Ashleigh said, glancing at her clipboard. "Then just walk him out."

"That's it?" Christina asked, shaking her head.

"That's all," Ashleigh replied.

"Whatever you say," Christina said, starting Star along the rail. She wasn't so sure it mattered if Star was in top shape for the Derby or not, anyway. If her mother's training schedule didn't ruin his chances in the race, her own state of mind would probably take care of it.

As Christina started Star along the rail, the colt seemed to feel her tension through the reins. He arched his neck and kicked, trying to get her to loosen the grip she had on the reins.

"I'm sorry, Star," she murmured, easing up a little. As they came around the far side of the track, she noticed a sports car pulling up near the barn, and a tall, dark-haired man emerged. She groaned to herself. What was Brad Townsend doing there?

Brad strode over to where Ashleigh stood at the rail, and as Christina and Star drew near she could hear their conversation.

"I just wanted to check out the competition," Brad said as Christina and Star trotted past.

"You've seen Star run," Ashleigh said mildly.

Brad said something else, but Star had moved far

enough down the track that Christina couldn't make out the words. She turned her head a little, trying to catch the rest of Brad's comments. At the same time she realized she wasn't focusing on Star. The colt snatched the bit and hauled the reins from her hands. Before she could collect him again, Star broke into a gallop, leaving Christina scrambling to keep her seat and regain control. Star was halfway around the track before she got him settled, and she felt her face burning with embarrassment at the display.

She sat straight in the saddle, keeping Star under close control as they finished the circuit.

Brad was shaking his head in disgust as they got closer. He looked from Christina to Star, then smiled coldly. "I guess I did the right thing unloading that colt," he said, loudly enough for Christina to hear him.

Christina felt herself go tense again, and Star responded immediately, his muscles bunching and his strides growing choppy as he fought Christina to let him run.

"Good luck with them," Brad went on, his voice still raised. "I always knew that colt wouldn't be any good, even if he does have some speed. But maybe with a different jockey, someone who could handle the pressure, he'd have a slight chance."

His words washed over Christina like a bucket of cold water. Before her mother could say anything else, Brad strode away. As he left the track Christina brought Star to the gap and jumped from his back.

"How could you stand there and let him talk about Star that way?" she fumed at her mother.

"Brad is all talk, Chris. You know that." Ashleigh glanced at the clipboard she was holding, then looked up at Christina. "You're going to let Brad's cheap little remarks get to you?" she asked, raising her eyebrows. "You should know better, Chris. He's kicking himself for letting Star go, even though he'd never admit it."

When Star had been deathly ill, Brad had signed Townsend Acres' interest in the colt over to Christina, thinking he was selling her a racehorse that wouldn't live to race again. Now Star was healthy and strong, and Brad was anything but happy about that.

Christina released an exasperated sigh. "All I know is that by not standing up for Star, you might as well be agreeing with Brad."

Ashleigh pinched her lips together. "I was not agreeing with Brad," she said tersely. "What has gotten into you, Christina?"

"Nothing," Christina said, leading Star away from the track. When she was out of earshot, she looked at

Star and made a face. "Nothing but my wreck with Raven, Melanie not talking to me, and trying to keep you geared up for the Derby while Mom is turning you into a lazy trail horse." She stroked Star's sweaty neck. "Other than that, nothing at all."

7

Ashleigh leaned on the rail of Star's paddock, enjoying the warmth of the late morning. The farm was quiet. All the horses had been taken care of, and Melanie and Christina were both at school. She watched Star amble across his pasture, pausing to nip at a bit of grass every few steps. The colt looked to be in perfect health. His rich chestnut coat gleamed in the April sun, and he reminded Ashleigh again of Pride as a young horse. She sighed, thinking of Christina's frustration and worry over the upcoming Derby.

She understood how Christina felt. No matter how carefully they planned and worked, racing was still a sport of chance. Star could be in perfect condition to run, but there were so many factors that affected the outcome of a horse race. Maybe racing Star before the Derby would help Christina, but Ashleigh didn't want to stress Star. She heaved a sigh of frustration, trying to think of something she could offer that would help both Christina and the colt.

"Star!" When she called his name, the colt popped his head up and looked at her for a moment. His regal pose, his build, and the intelligent warmth in his eyes made her think of Pride again.

That had been so many years ago, and everyone had been so sure of Pride's ability to take the Triple Crown despite the challenging schedule of races Clay Townsend had set up for him. Everyone, that was, except Charlie Burke.

Star dropped his nose into the thick bluegrass again, and Ashleigh felt the memories of that long-past time sweep over her once more. . . .

"Just look at him," Clay Townsend said, leaning his elbows on the top rail of the pasture fence. "He looks like he never ran the Derby."

Ashleigh took a step closer to Clay, gazing at Pride. The chestnut colt stood proudly in the middle of the grassy pasture, staring into the distance. She nodded silently. Pride had recovered rapidly from the speed duel with Count Abdul, and as far as Ashleigh could tell, he was already geared up for the Preakness.

"He does look great," she agreed, admiring Pride's glistening coat and his alert stance. "I'm getting excited about racing him at Pimlico."

"It would be a real feather in the Townsend Acres cap if Pride won the second jewel of the Triple Crown," Clay said.

Beside Ashleigh, Charlie grunted quietly. Ashleigh shot him a quick look. The old trainer looked troubled, but with Clay there, Ashleigh wasn't about to ask him what was bothering him.

"When you run him next week," Clay continued, "it would be very impressive if you could get the same kind of speed he showed at Churchill Downs."

Ashleigh stared at Clay, startled by the comment. "He wore himself out running the way he did," she said.

"He looks great right now," Clay responded. "I'm confident in this colt. If he could sweep the field again, Townsend Acres' reputation for breeding exceptional winners would be known worldwide."

Ashleigh turned her attention from Clay back to Pride. She knew Clay was worried about Townsend Acres' financial situation, but he sounded as though he was quoting Brad, who didn't care one bit about

Pride's well-being. The colt dropped his head and began grazing as the sun sent warm light over his red-gold coat. Pride looked as if he was illuminated, glowing in the late spring sunshine, and Ashleigh felt her heart bursting with love for the beautiful horse. If Pride could win the Preakness as dramatically as he had the Derby, it would bring a lot of good publicity not only to Townsend Acres but to Whitebrook as well.

"We need to keep the colt's well-being in mind," Charlie said softly. "He may look perfectly fit, but the last several races have taken their toll on his stamina."

"Maybe the way you've been working him between races isn't benefiting him," Brad Townsend said, snotty as ever. Clay's tall, dark-haired son stood at Clay's other shoulder, flashing Charlie his usual look of disgust. "You've been coddling him like he's some old veteran. And putting that little redheaded girl on him isn't doing the colt any favors. He needs an exercise rider who knows what he's doing."

Ashleigh tensed at Brad's condescending words. She, too, wanted to push Pride a little harder on the practice track, but Charlie was being very cautious in exercising the racehorse. Samantha kept his works slow and steady, keeping in mind that Pride needed to build up fresh reserves of energy for the next grueling race in the Triple Crown series.

Clay looked from Brad to Charlie. "Is there some-one else better qualified to work the colt?" he asked. "We don't want to spoil Pride's chances of winning the Preakness."

Charlie pulled his hat off and clenched it in his fists. "Sammy is doing a fine job with the horse," he said evenly. "She understands him better than anyone, and she's doing just what I've instructed her to do."

Clay nodded thoughtfully, then turned to Ash-leigh. "As half owner of the animal, I do have some concerns about how he's being prepared for the race. I'd like to have him over at Townsend Acres until it's time to ship him to Baltimore for the Preakness."

"That's a bad idea," Ashleigh said quickly. She was certain Brad had been talking to Clay, trying to con-vince his father to take control of Pride's training. She knew Clay's financial concerns were affecting his judgment, and Brad had surely used that to his advan-tage. He would have loved to get Pride away from Whitebrook and have Townsend Acres be able to claim all the credit for the colt's successes.

"We have better facilities and a real trainer," Brad said rudely.

Ashleigh felt Charlie bristle beside her, and she tilted her head to glare at the younger Townsend. "We have a fine practice track here," she responded, keeping her voice level. "And Charlie has proven himself to be one of the best trainers in Kentucky."

Brad shrugged and glanced at his father. "Racehorses aren't what they were thirty years ago," he said, ignoring Ashleigh's cold look. "Pride's win in the Derby could have been a fluke. We don't want to risk a failure in the Preakness."

Clay worked his jaw, gazing intently at the colt, who had wandered across the pasture. The muscles in Pride's sleek rump rippled under his coat as he ambled through the lush grass, taking a bite here and there as he moved.

"He does look good right now," Clay said, "but Brad is right. We don't want to take a chance of missing some step in his training."

Ashleigh's heart was torn. The pressure of winning the Preakness weighed heavily on her. Was there something more they could do at Townsend Acres? She thought about the wonderful track Clay had installed, of the beautiful facilities and all the staff he had around the barn. She didn't want to deprive Pride of every advantage he could be given. But she knew deep down that sending Pride over to Townsend Acres would be a mistake.

She shook her head firmly. "We've got everything Pride needs right here," she replied. Being handled by

Samantha was the best thing they could give Pride. Samantha lavished attention on the colt, and he responded by doing his best for her on the track and being relaxed and contented when she was around him. The only thing Townsend Acres had to offer was a fancier facility.

"Well," Clay said slowly, sounding rather unconvinced, "if he doesn't pull off a win at the Preakness, we'll have this discussion again." He sighed and frowned at Ashleigh. "I hope you know what you're doing."

"I do," Ashleigh said quickly, then glanced toward Charlie and smiled firmly. "*We* do."

After Clay and Brad left the farm, Ashleigh followed Charlie into the barn, her own turmoil over working the colt and racing in the Preakness tumbling about her heart and mind.

"Do you think Clay may be right?" she asked Charlie.

The trainer narrowed his eyes and shook his head. "I think Clay has been listening to Brad too much," he said sourly. "I don't want you to let Pride push himself as hard as he did in the last race. I'm afraid we're going to wear him down. If that happens, you'll have an exhausted horse with no spirit for running anything, let alone a hard race."

Ashleigh sighed, then nodded. "So what do we do?" she asked.

"Trust me to keep him on the right schedule," Charlie said. "Samantha is taking the best possible care of him. You just need to do the same when you race him."

The week before the Preakness, Samantha spent every spare minute she had treating Pride like royalty. Ashleigh felt sure the colt was going to be in fine condition for the race, and when they headed for the track at Pimlico a few days before the Preakness, she gave Samantha a warm hug. "Thanks for doing so much for Pride," she said. "He looks perfect, and it's all thanks to you."

"We'll see you up there on Friday night," Samantha replied, giving Pride's sleek nose a loving pet before she loaded him into the horse trailer.

Pride settled into his stall at Pimlico quickly, and Ashleigh was eager to take him onto the track to get him mentally relaxed as well. But when it started to rain, she felt her spirits sink a little. "It had better stop before Saturday," she groaned to Charlie. They stood under the overhang in front of Pride's stall, watching a heavy downpour soak the ground.

Charlie shook his head. "We can't control the weather, missy," he said. "If it's sloppy on Saturday, we'll have mud caulks put on the colt, but that's all we can do. Just don't run him into an injury. Better a sound loser than a crippled winner."

She nodded in agreement but glanced over her shoulder to where Pride was tearing a bite of hay from the net hanging in his stall. *Better a sound winner*, she thought.

On Saturday the track was still heavy and wet. "Watch Carousel Delight," Charlie told Ashleigh as she handed him her racing saddle. "That colt has a reputation for running well on an off track, and he could surprise us all."

"Got it," Ashleigh said, heading for the viewing paddock. She smoothed the front of her green-and-gold Townsend Acres silks, thinking forward to a day when she would wear Whitebrook colors instead. *It won't be long,* she promised herself.

Clay Townsend stood at the number five spot, which matched the gate number Pride had drawn for the Preakness. Brad and Lavinia were with him, but when Ashleigh joined the threesome to wait for Samantha to bring Pride around, only Clay nodded and smiled at her.

Lavinia lifted her chin, looked down her nose at Ashleigh for a split second, then turned her attention back to Brad.

Ashleigh watched Pride come around the paddock, his gait light and his head high. Her love for the big horse swelled in her chest as she watched him move.

"He looks excellent," Clay commented as Samantha stopped the colt in front of them. "Get more of that speed out of him today, Ashleigh. Let's see another two-length lead at the end of the race."

Ashleigh offered Clay a thin, tense smile, then sprang onto Pride's back, settling in place as Samantha led them to the pony rider.

Once they were in the gate, Pride snorted softly, sniffing the metal sides of the chute as Ashleigh prepared herself for the start.

When the bell clanged, they joined the wall of horses and riders blasting from the starting gate. Ashleigh crouched over Pride's shoulders, focusing on the expanse of track in front of them. With horses on both sides, Pride and Ashleigh were quickly splattered with the mud that flew from the animals' pounding hooves.

Pride ran strongly, holding the front line in spite of the heavy footing on the track. Ultrasound, the colt who had been a constant threat to them throughout the spring, ran well, pushing Pride's lead. Ashleigh darted a look under her arm, trying to spot Carousel Delight, the horse Charlie had warned her about.

As they came through the turn, the black colt hadn't moved up from the crowd of horses, but when they reached the stretch, she glanced back again to see Carousel Delight's jockey lean forward and apply his whip to the colt's hip.

Carousel Delight surged forward, passing several horses in one bold move, then closed in on Ultrasound.

Ashleigh leaned forward, kneading her knuckles into Pride's neck. He felt strong and steady under her, and she knew she had to push him. She needed to ask him to give everything he had if they hoped to win the Preakness.

"Let's go!" she cried, holding her weight off the colt's back as she asked him for more speed.

Pride stretched out and increased his speed, but Ashleigh could feel the toll it was taking on him. She glanced back again to see Carousel Delight challenging their lead. She sucked in a deep breath, then gave Pride's hip a tap with the whip she carried.

Pride dug in deeper, finding a little more speed, and the chestnut colt crossed the finish line first, winning the Preakness by one length. It took little effort to slow him, and by the time Samantha took hold of his bridle, Ashleigh knew the race had drained the colt's last ounce of energy. Could he get it back before the Belmont?

After the winner's circle ceremony, Ashleigh hurried to the backside to check on Pride. The thrill of winning the race was dimmed a little when she saw just how exhausted the colt looked.

"He's wiped out," Charlie said grimly.

Pride walked slowly as Samantha cooled him out, barely able to lift his hooves. His eyes were listless and vacant, and Ashleigh swallowed a lump in her throat. Pride might have won the race, but what had she done to him, asking him to give so much?

A nudge on Ashleigh's shoulder stirred her from her memory, and when she looked up, Star was at the fence, running his nose along her forearm.

"You want some special attention, don't you?" she asked, giving his forehead a gentle rub.

Star bobbed his head, and Ashleigh smiled fondly at the colt. "Christina will be home from school before too long," she promised. "I'm sure she'll have a few treats for you."

Star gave up trying to entice Ashleigh to give him some special goodies and went back to grazing. Ashleigh left him alone. She headed back to the barn to review Star's training schedule. Star wasn't being asked to work nearly as hard as Pride had. Maybe she was being a little overprotective of the colt, but she had to trust her own judgment. She would never put another horse through the intense pressure they had put on Pride. Star's health needed to be protected, and she was going to make sure he was given the best possible care. Christina might not believe it, but Ashleigh was determined to do everything she knew how to do to keep Star on top of his game and give him the chance to win all three races in the Triple Crown.

8

"Chris, will you stop by the office when you're done with Raven?" Mike asked Christina early Saturday morning. The morning works were finished and all the horses were in their paddocks, except for Raven.

"Okay." Christina made one more pass across Raven's shoulder with the brush she held and gave her father a quizzical look, but Mike was already walking away.

Christina returned her attention to the black filly. Raven still looked listless, her eyes dull and her head drooping. Her weight was dropping, but Dr. Seymour insisted on keeping her medicated so that she would stand quietly. It tore at Christina's heart to see the filly trapped in her stall, her weight supported by the sling, her injured leg heavily bandaged.

Dr. Seymour wouldn't offer them any real hope for her recovery. "All we can do is wait and see," he would say, shaking his head sadly. "She doesn't seem to be coping very well with her confinement."

Christina finished grooming the filly and picked up her bucket of tools. "Of course you don't like being confined, but you have to get better," she murmured to Raven, giving the filly's nose a stroke before she left the stall.

When she went into the office, her father was talking on the phone, scheduling a mare for a breeding to Jazzman, Star's sire. Mike allowed only a limited number of mares to be bred to the horse, and spent more time turning people down than scheduling mares to come to Whitebrook. Christina moved a stack of *Bloodhorse* magazines from a chair and sat down, waiting for him to finish.

When he finally hung up the phone he smiled at her. "Star's successes certainly have made Jazzman very popular," he said, chuckling. "If Star wins the Derby, we'll have to get an answering service to deal with all the requests for breedings."

"What did you want me for?" Christina asked, eager to get off the subject of Star running in the Derby.

"I need you to run over to Keeneland," her father said, picking a slip of paper off the desk. He held it out to her. "We went in with a couple of other owners and ordered some new tack. It was delivered to the Keeneland track today, and your mother is like a kid at Christmas. She wants to see her new toys."

Christina nodded. "I should probably change my clothes," she said, indicating her grubby jeans and T-shirt. She knew she didn't need to dress up to go to the track, but her barn clothes weren't in the best shape.

Her father shrugged. "You always look fine to me," he said, holding the receipt out to her.

"Thanks, Dad," Christina said, then hurried to the house to pull on some clean clothes. When she reached the front door, she ran into Melanie, who was heading out.

"Hey," Christina said, pausing on the porch. "Do you want to go for a drive?"

Instead of replying, Melanie gave her a cold look and walked past her, down the steps and along the path that led to the barn.

Christina watched her go. Obviously Melanie wasn't ready to forgive her. Christina was afraid that if Raven had to be put down, they would never get past this, and she missed their friendship so badly. She let out a heavy sigh, forgetting all about changing her clothes, and walked over to the Blazer. She spent the whole half-hour ride to Keeneland trying to figure out a way to work things out with Melanie. But by the time she pulled the Blazer into an empty parking space at the track's backside she still didn't have any answers.

When she walked through the gate, the backside was relatively quiet. There were no meets going at this time of year, but there were some jockeys and trainers talking near the track office. Christina recognized a few of them, but no one even glanced in her direction as she walked by. She headed for the office, intent on getting her parents' package and heading home.

She looked up at the sound of thundering hooves on the track and saw the Townsends' gray colt, Celtic Mist, galloping out of the turn. The colt looked magnificent, his gait strong and his mane blowing back as his exercise rider guided him beside the rail. She sighed. Celtic Mist was going to be tough to beat.

She started to turn toward the office again when she spotted tall, dark-haired Parker Townsend striding away from the track stables. Her heart squeezed at the sight of him. Because both of them had busy schedules, they had agreed not to keep seeing each other, but that didn't make her feelings for Parker any less strong. She took a step in his direction, biting her lip. It would be nice to spend a little time visiting with him. Parker would understand her dismay over Raven's injury and Melanie's anger toward her, and he'd support her the way he always did. But Parker was focused on the track rail, and Christina stopped, following his gaze.

She frowned automatically when she saw Brad Townsend, Parker's father, standing near the rail, deep in conversation with a track official. Parker's mother, Lavinia, stood beside Brad, talking to a petite girl with dark, curly hair. The girl looked to be about Christina's age, and Lavinia was smiling down at her, seeming very intent on something the girl was saying.

Suddenly acutely aware of her grungy clothes and disheveled appearance, Christina stayed where she was and held back from calling out to Parker. Even though she would have loved to talk to him, the last people in the world she wanted to see were Brad and Lavinia. She didn't want to hear any more of Brad's rude comments, and she didn't want to hear any of Lavinia's catty remarks, either.

As she watched, the girl Lavinia was talking to looked up and saw Parker. She waved excitedly, then hurried to Parker's side. Christina's breath caught as the girl grabbed Parker's arm and tugged him toward his parents. Parker smiled warmly at her, letting her drag him toward Brad and Lavinia.

Tears came to Christina's eyes, and her stomach seemed to sink down to her toes. But when Brad turned away from the track official and gave the girl a friendly smile, Christina realized that her stomach was somehow able to sink even lower. She had never gotten along with Parker's parents. The Townsends had never forgotten that her grandparents had been employees at Townsend Acres, and Brad jumped at every opportunity to belittle Ashleigh and Mike. As a teenager, Brad had been furious at his father for giving Ashleigh an interest in Wonder, and he had made a point of giving the Reeses as much trouble as he could over the training and racing of her offspring.

Christina knew she should tear her eyes away, but she continued to watch as Parker and the girl carried on an animated conversation. It looked as if Parker had bonded more closely with his parents after he and Christina had broken up, and found a girlfriend they approved of. When Lavinia reached over to tuck a curl behind the girl's ear, it was finally too much for Christina. She turned away and hurried into the office.

She waited impatiently at the counter to show her receipt and pick up her parents' tack, struggling with how much Parker's betrayal hurt. She loaded the box of racing saddles and bridles into the Blazer, then sat in the parking lot for a few minutes, feeling as though her world were crumbling around her. Finally she started the SUV and headed for Whitebrook.

When she arrived at the farm, the house was quiet.

She stopped in the kitchen to grab a carrot from the refrigerator, then went down to the barn to check on Raven and Star. Raven raised her head and nickered softly when Christina walked up to her stall. It was enough to give Christina's spirits a small lift.

"You must be feeling better," she said, offering the filly a chunk of carrot. But Raven ignored the treat. Instead she shifted her weight in the sling, wiggling impatiently at her restraints. Christina petted the filly, trying to soothe her. She froze when she noticed how soft Raven's muscles felt already. "I don't know how they expect you to start walking after you've been like this for so many days," she said. But she knew that in order for Raven to heal she had to keep the weight off her leg, which was also part of the risk of trying to save the filly.

When Raven tossed her head and tried to take a step, Christina felt a rush of worry that she would fight to get free of her bonds. But she also felt a flicker of hope that Raven was feeling well enough to want to move.

She left Raven after checking her water, then headed for Star's paddock. The colt whinnied when he saw her and galloped to the fence, skidding to a stop in front of Christina.

"Here you go," she said, feeding the carrot chunks

to the colt. "It won't be too long before you get to run again," she promised him, smiling when he flung his head up and snorted. "We both need to get into the right frame of mind if we're going to show the world what a wonder horse you are," she told him, reaching up to tease the silky soft end of his nose.

After she spent a few more minutes with Star she went back up to the house. It was a good time to get her homework done. She carried her books to her room and settled down at her desk, opening her World Problems textbook to read the latest assignment. She tried to immerse herself in the dry text, but her mind kept wandering to Raven's injury, Parker's new girl-friend, and the upcoming Derby.

When she heard the phone ring, Christina jumped up and headed for the stairs. Halfway down she heard Melanie answer the phone. Christina hesitated on the stairs, waiting to see if the call was for her.

"Hi, Jazz," she heard Melanie say. Her shoulders sagged when she realized the call wasn't for her, and she turned to walk back up to her room.

"You won't believe what happened while we were in Florida," she heard Melanie say, then there was a long pause.

Christina hesitated, feeling a little guilty about eavesdropping, but she couldn't resist listening.

"Chris screwed up in a race and caused an accident. Raven is hurt so badly, she might need to be put down."

After another pause, she heard Melanie make a disgusted sound.

"She wasn't paying attention," Melanie said with disdain. "She ruined a wonderful horse."

Christina felt her heart shrink at Melanie's harsh words. She slipped back upstairs and tried to keep studying, but her concentration was shot. She closed the textbook and went downstairs, making sure she made lots of noise so that Melanie would know she was in the house. By the time she reached the kitchen, the phone was back in its cradle and Melanie was nowhere to be seen.

Christina headed down to the barn, trying to shake the deep feeling of loss over her friendship with her cousin and her relationship with Parker. When she reached the aisle where Raven was being kept, she saw Melanie in her stall, trying to get the filly to eat a few treats. But Raven showed little interest in the carrot chunks and apple slices. Christina watched, guilt-stricken, as Melanie put her arms around the horse's dark neck and started to cry. Christina turned the other way, heading out to Star's paddock instead. She couldn't face Melanie now.

After so many arguments with her mother over Star, seeing Parker with his new girlfriend, and hearing Melanie's conversation with Jazz, Christina couldn't help wondering if anything was ever going to go right for her again.

9

The second Christina got home from school on Monday, she headed straight to the barn, where Dr. Seymour's Land Cruiser was parked near the open door. She hurried inside, her hands clenched into tense fists. *Please let Raven be fine*, she kept repeating to herself as she walked down the aisle.

When she neared Raven's stall, Dr. Seymour was packing up his equipment and preparing to leave. Mike, Ashleigh, and Ian were standing near the filly's stall. Christina held her breath as she looked at their faces, trying to muster hope, but their expressions were all serious.

"I just don't see that she's healing well," Dr. Seymour said. "I don't know how much longer it's going to take before we will even know if she can bear weight on that leg."

Mike and Ashleigh exchanged a solemn glance. "How long can we keep her like this?" Ashleigh asked. "Do you—do you think we should put her down?"

No! She couldn't let that happen. "She's been trying to walk on it," Christina jumped in, desperate. "Maybe she knows it's well enough for her to use it. Why don't you let her try?"

Dr. Seymour gave her a sympathetic smile. "I know you want her to be all right, Chris, but even if she could keep weight on the leg, at this point not enough time has passed for the tendon to fuse to the bone." He glanced back at Raven and shook his head. "She's getting impatient with being trapped in her stall, but that doesn't mean she's getting any better. I'm sorry, Chris. We're doing the best we can for her."

"Let's hang on a while longer," Mike said to the vet. "I'd like to give her as much time as we possibly can."

"That's your call," Dr. Seymour said, picking up his bag. "I'll be back in a couple of days."

After Dr. Seymour left the barn, Christina got a wheelbarrow and began cleaning Raven's stall. Ashleigh watched her for a few minutes, then followed Ian and Mike, who were on their way to the stallion barn.

Raven grunted softly at Christina as she removed

the soiled bedding. Christina paused to rub Raven's neck. "You have to be patient," Christina admonished the filly. "Please just rest quietly so you get a good chance to heal." But even as she was speaking, Raven tried to turn in the hated sling.

"I'm so sorry, Raven," she murmured, giving the filly's neck a gentle pet. "I never would have put you in danger on purpose."

Raven leaned her head against Christina, who massaged the base of the filly's ears, wishing she knew some way to make the injured horse whole again. "I'll check on you again later," she told Raven. She filled the filly's water bucket and tucked a flake of hay in her hay net, then got Star's halter from the tack room.

When she walked out to his paddock, Star was pacing along the fence line. As soon as he caught sight of her, the colt trotted to where she was climbing between the rails. He nudged at her impatiently as she slipped his halter over his nose.

"Maybe a trail ride will make both of us feel better," she told him as she led him toward the barn. Star tossed his head and tugged at the crossties while Christina got his tack out. He pawed the barn floor and danced his hindquarters around while she saddled him, and as soon as she was on his back the colt began prancing in place. Christina sat deeply in the saddle and kept a firm hold on the reins.

"We're going for a trail ride," she reminded him. "And we're not supposed to go any faster than a slow jog, so don't get any ideas about a gallop."

Star settled down a little as they rode away from the barns, but he still moved out eagerly, trying to break out of a walk. When they reached the trails, he sniffed the air and jumped around skittishly. Christina rubbed his neck gently, trying to soothe the excited horse.

She was relieved when they started along the trail and Star quieted down somewhat. Soon he was walking steadily, although she could still feel the energy humming in his muscles with every stride.

"What am I going to do, Star?" Christina sat straight in the saddle, feeling the gentle rocking of Star's movements as they followed the tree-lined trail. The afternoon sun filtered through the broad leaves of the maple and oak trees that hung over the path, scattering broken bits of light across the colt's shiny mane.

"Melanie came into the barn this morning and saw me grooming Raven," Christina sighed. "I didn't know if she was going to start yelling at me or start crying. But she isn't the only one who's upset. I wish she could understand how bad I feel about Raven. I mean, doesn't she see that it hurts me as much as it does her to see Raven so frail?"

Star continued walking, flicking his ears to catch the sounds of the birds in the trees. Christina reached out to pat the colt's sleek neck. Star might be able to communicate his wants and needs to her, but he couldn't give her any answers about how to deal with Melanie.

"The vet says we still have to wait several more days before we'll know if the surgery helped Raven or not."

Star tugged at the reins a little, and Christina smiled at the message he was sending, but she shook her head. "Forget it, fellow," she said. "Mom was very clear. Walk a lot, jog a little, and nothing more." She heaved another sigh and swatted a low-hanging branch out of her way. "I hope she knows what she's doing, turning you into an easygoing trail horse."

Star dropped his nose to nip at a clump of weeds, and Christina squeezed her legs a little, urging him on. "Don't you dare taste that," she scolded him gently. "All we need now is for you to poison yourself on a piece of fern."

A little stream meandered close to the trail, and Christina watched the clear water bubble over the rocky bottom, forming tiny rapids and swirls. From overhead, a squirrel scolded at them as they passed under his tree. Christina felt her tension start to fade a little as the quiet of the woods and the soft gurgling of the water soothed her senses.

After several more minutes Star dropped his head and plodded quietly along the path. "You're getting pretty relaxed, too, aren't you?" Christina asked him, admiring the play of muscles in his powerful shoulders. "But we still need to do something to get you pumped up. I don't want you to get onto the track for the Derby with the idea that it's going to be just another trail ride."

After another hour of easy riding, she turned Star toward home. As they neared the farm, the training track came into view. Christina pulled Star to a stop and watched Dani cantering Catwink along the outside rail of the track. Star caught sight of the activity, and his head sprang up. His ears pricked forward, and Christina felt his body tense under her.

She quickly collected the reins, holding him still. "Forget it, big guy," she said, although she was relieved at the sudden excitement she felt in his reaction to seeing activity on the track. Even the leisurely trail ride hadn't dampened his eagerness to run. "Mom would put us both out to pasture if she saw us gallop down to the track."

She walked Star down the path, keeping him at a prancing walk. When they returned to the barn,

Christina groomed the colt thoroughly, then fed him a generous flake of hay and a can of grain, sprinkling supplements over the feed before she set it in front of him. "Eat it all," she ordered the colt, pleased when he eagerly plunged his nose into the grain. The trail ride seemed to have stimulated his appetite, and he was relaxed enough that he stood quietly in his stall, not acting antsy about getting out of the small space.

The next morning, after her session with Star on the track, Christina put the colt in his pasture and climbed into the Blazer. Instead of going straight to school, she headed in the opposite direction. In twenty minutes she turned up a long driveway, past a large sign that informed visitors they were at Tall Oaks Farm.

She parked next to Cindy McLean's car in front of the caretaker's cottage. She climbed from the SUV and paused to look around Tall Oaks' grounds. The main house, a Civil War–era mansion built of brick, sat on a rise overlooking rolling green pastures. The cottage where Cindy lived was tiny compared to the house, but it was similar in style and had the same gracious charm as the mansion.

"Over here, Chris!" She turned to see Cindy standing in the doorway of one of Tall Oaks' large, well-built barns. Christina crossed the yard, admiring the new footing on the practice track and noting the repairs that had been done since Ben al-Rihani had taken over the farm during the winter.

"Everything looks so nice here," she commented when she reached Cindy.

Cindy, Ian and Beth McLean's adopted daughter, had been a jockey in New York for several years until injury forced her to retire from racing. When Ben al-Rihani had bought Tall Oaks from the descendants of the original owners, he brought his own Thoroughbreds from Dubai to train and race in the United States. Now Cindy was working as the head trainer at the estate.

"Ben's making sure everything here is perfect," Cindy said happily, pointing at a new building being constructed on the grounds. "We're putting in an indoor arena for training foals."

"That's going to be great," Christina said, gazing at the large building.

"I'm having so much fun getting everything set up here," Cindy said, then gestured for Christina to follow her into the barn. "Come see Champion."

"Oh, I can't wait—I was four years old the last time I saw him," Christina said. Ben's father had bought the stallion and taken him to Dubai, and Ben had just recently brought Champion back to the United States.

When Cindy stopped in front of a luxurious box

stall, a chestnut stallion poked his head out of the stall and nickered softly.

"Hello, Champion," Christina said, reaching up to give the horse's jaw a soft pet. Champion, like Star, was one of Wonder's foals, and the relationship between the two horses was obvious in the shape of their heads and their glorious red-gold coats.

"He's so happy to be back in Kentucky," Cindy said, rubbing Champion's elegant forehead. Cindy leaned into the stall to give Champion's glossy neck a loving pat, and the stallion lipped affectionately at her blond hair.

"How is Gratis doing?" Christina asked. "Is he all geared up for the Derby?"

"He's ready to run," Cindy said proudly. When Ben had purchased Tall Oaks, he had also bought all the horses belonging to the farm, including Khan, the farm's prized stallion, and Gratis, the strong-willed bay colt Cindy was training for the Derby.

Christina had raced the recalcitrant colt several times during the winter, proving herself to several trainers who saw how well she could handle a difficult horse. Of course, now Gratis's racing skill could be a problem for Christina instead of an advantage, since he'd be competition for Star at the Derby.

"Come on out to the track," Cindy said. "He's starting his morning work right now." Cindy led the way out of the barn and to the rail of the practice track, where an exercise rider was working Gratis on the track. For a minute Christina watched the massive bay colt fight the rider, trying to get his own way.

Christina smiled, remembering how hard Gratis had been to handle until she learned to read him.

Cindy turned to Christina. "Did you come over just to check out the competition?" she asked in a teasing voice.

"No," Christina said. "I just came over to visit." She watched Gratis start to wheel around on the track, and waited for the exercise rider to fly off the colt's back. Instead the rider took control of the colt's movements and urged him forward. Christina was impressed. It had taken her several spills before she learned to control Gratis and prevent him from pulling one of his stunts.

"Who's that guy riding him?" she asked Cindy. Gratis was jogging nicely now, as though he had never given a thought to dumping his rider.

"A kid who calls himself Wolf," Cindy said dryly. Obviously Cindy wasn't a big fan of his, but Christina couldn't see why not.

"He seems to have Gratis figured out," Christina commented.

Cindy shrugged. "I guess he's doing okay," she said. "I'd rather be doing it myself, though."

Christina nodded in understanding. "It must be hard to have to stand here and watch other people working the racehorses," she said.

"I had my turn," Cindy said, "but it's hard to let go of riding after it was my life for so many years."

Christina rested her forearms on the rail and watched the big bay colt shift into a smooth gallop. She knew how Cindy felt. She wished she could be out there herself, galloping Star. At least the accident with Raven hadn't made a dent in her instinctive urge to ride. And she had been feeling a little less nervous recently with Star. Maybe Ashleigh had been right about her needing to put the wreck behind her and concentrate on the Derby. But it was still hard when she saw Raven every day, dealing with the injury that Christina had caused.

"How is Raven doing?" Cindy asked in a concerned voice, as if sensing Christina's thoughts. "What does the vet say?"

Christina kept her eyes on Gratis. "We don't know yet," she admitted, then cast a quick glance at Cindy. "He won't say how long it's going to take before she's healed enough to try walking."

Cindy nodded, her attention returning to the horse and rider on the track. "Take him up a bit," she called, watching closely as the rider gave her a cold look before he slowed the colt to a jog and kept him to the outside rail. "I should be on Gratis," she muttered. "I hate trying to tell someone else how to handle a horse." She rolled her left shoulder and shook her head. "Oh, well," she said, smiling thinly, "I'm not a jockey anymore." She turned back to Christina. "What about you? Are you all pumped up about the Derby?"

Christina grimaced. "I guess so, but I don't know how I feel about running Star in the Derby anymore, after what happened with Raven."

Cindy frowned, her brow furrowing. "You know, Chris," she said, "you've got it all mixed up."

Christina looked back at her in confusion. "What do you mean?" she asked.

"If you use this as an excuse to not race Star, or if you let it hold you back, you'll be throwing away the greatest chance of your life over a little accident."

"It wasn't a little accident," Christina protested. "Raven still might have to be put down."

"It happens," Cindy said shortly. She looked at Gratis again, then nodded thoughtfully as the rider headed the big colt toward the gap in the rail. "He sure moves well," she commented, more to herself than to Christina. She waved at the rider. "After you've cooled him out, wrap his legs," she called.

The rider hopped from the colt's back and glared at

Cindy. "I know how to take care of him," he replied, then led the sweat-soaked horse away.

"That guy makes me nuts," Cindy grumbled. She glanced at Christina again. "You know, for all the hard work and all the years I put into racing, I never did get a chance to ride in any of the Triple Crown races," she said. "I can't offer you any pre-Derby advice or give you any training secrets. Everything I know, I learned from my dad and your mom. You have the best people around to help you prepare Star, and yourself."

Christina couldn't help rolling her eyes at that, thinking of her mother's ridiculous caution with Star.

Cindy raised her eyebrows. "That was the sourest look I've ever seen on your face, Chris. What's really the matter? You may be a little nervous after the accident with Raven, but there's something else, isn't there?"

Christina inhaled deeply. "Mom is being so careful with Star," she finally said. "She won't even let me breeze him until a few days before the Derby. Poor Star thinks he's retired. I know we're going to end up blowing the race."

Cindy worked her jaw a little, then looked at Christina intently. "Your mother knows exactly what she's doing," she said. "Ask her about overworking a horse sometime. Ask her about Pride."

"I know all about Pride," Christina replied. "But why is everyone so sure that Mom's experience with him is going to help Star?"

Cindy narrowed her eyes. "Charlie Burke taught your mom how to train a winning racehorse," she said. "Without Charlie's experience, Pride never would have done as well as he did. Maybe you should give your mom some credit for what she's learned over the years."

"I don't think it's fair to compare Pride's situation to Star's," Christina said. "Star hasn't had to work nearly as hard as Pride did."

"But he was at least as worn down from that virus he had," Cindy countered. "Remember, I helped nurse him back to health. That colt was in bad shape, Chris. I suggest you go talk to your mother and quit feeling sorry for yourself." She paused, then smiled softly. "I spent enough years feeling sorry for myself to know it doesn't accomplish anything. You need to have some faith in your mom, in your horse, and in yourself." Cindy glanced at her watch. "Right now, though, don't you think you'd better get to school?"

Christina looked at her own watch and gasped. "I'll see you later," she said, turning to hurry to the Blazer. The last thing she needed now was to miss her first-period class.

While she drove, Christina thought about what Cindy had said. As hard as it was to admit it, maybe Cindy was right. By the time she reached the high school, Christina knew what she had to do. To start with, she and Melanie both needed to concentrate on getting their horses ready for the Derby *together*. That was always how they worked best. Which meant it was time to clear the air between them. So the first step was figuring out how she was going to accomplish that.

10

Christina's frustration grew by the second as she watched Melanie gallop Image on the practice track. *How can Mom let her work her horse like that and keep Star from doing the same thing?* she fumed to herself. Melanie's expression was intense as she kept Image to the inside rail, leaning forward over the filly's withers.

Image looked fantastic. Christina wondered how Star would be after not having run hard for so many weeks. Why couldn't her mother see that Star needed a hard gallop, too? She turned to Ashleigh, who stood beside her at the rail, watching Image as well.

But before she could say a word, Ashleigh shook her head. "I know what you're going to say," she said. "And the answer is still no. Image hasn't had the problems Star had. She doesn't need to be handled as lightly."

Christina gritted her teeth. "He's fine, Mom," she said. "Why do you keep insisting he's too fragile to have a good, hard workout?"

"Because I want to be sure we do what's best for him," Ashleigh replied.

Christina stalked away from the track, trying to contain her irritation. She would never understand her mother. She went into the barn, where Dani had just put Star up. Ashleigh didn't even want Star and Image on the track together because she didn't want Star getting overstimulated. Christina had worked the colt before the other racehorses went onto the track for their morning works.

"He hardly even broke a sweat today," Dani commented, handing Christina a can of grain.

"I know," Christina said, trying not to let her annoyance show.

"The Derby is getting close, so maybe your mom will start pushing him now," Dani said, stuffing hay into a hay net for Star.

"I don't know what her plans are," Christina replied, picking up the hay net to take to Star.

When she got to the colt's stall, Star had his nose in the aisle. He whinnied eagerly when he saw her.

"Here you go, Star," Christina said, pouring the can of grain into his feed pan. "Even if you can't burn it off by running, you can at least keep your weight and energy up."

Ashleigh had increased Star's grain ration after she and Ian had agreed that the colt's weight was down. "Just watch him closely," Ashleigh had warned Christina. "We don't want him getting fat."

Star shoved his nose into the grain and began eating greedily. Christina rested her elbows on the stall wall and watched him for a while, then walked down to Raven's stall. The filly grunted softly, and Christina petted her nose. Raven lipped at her fingers, and Christina smiled. "I'll be right back," she promised, turning to head for the feed room to get a handful of grain for the filly.

As she turned she almost ran into Melanie. She froze, staring at her cousin's angry expression.

"What are you doing here?" Melanie demanded bitterly. "Why don't you just leave Raven alone?"

Christina's stomach churned, and suddenly she felt her own anger build. "You have to stop blaming me," she said sharply. "It was an accident. I never would have hurt Raven, and you know it."

"You were probably so wrapped up in thinking about Star, as always, that you didn't pay any attention to what was going on with the race you were in on the track," Melanie snapped.

Before Christina could say anything else, Melanie turned and stalked out of the barn. Christina heard the engine of the Blazer roar to life. She hurried to the barn door in time to see Melanie speed down the driveway. Christina slumped against the side of the barn. Were things ever going to get better with Melanie? She had to figure out some way to make Melanie understand how bad she felt and how much she cared about Raven.

She looked out over the paddocks at the grazing horses. The Thoroughbreds seemed so peaceful, wandering through the lush pastures, nibbling at the rich bluegrass. A sense of calmness filled her as she gazed at the beautiful animals, and an idea sprang to mind. She knew what she could give Melanie that might help. She had to give it a try, anyway.

Christina walked through the barns until she found her mother in the stallion barn. She was standing in front of Pride's stall, talking to George Ballard, the stallion manager. Christina hurried up the aisle, pausing briefly to pat Jazzman's nose when the black horse shoved his head toward her. She avoided Terminator, who flattened his ears to his head and bared his teeth when she passed his stall, then stopped at March to Glory's stall to give the gray horse a quick rub on the nose.

Her mother glanced up when Christina reached Pride's stall, but her attention was on George, who held a sheaf of papers in his hand.

"I think it would be a good idea to add a new row of stalls to the barn where we keep the mares brought in for breeding," George said, pointing at a column of numbers on the top page. "With the number of stallions we have, we're going to be overbooked for the mares' barn next spring."

Ashleigh nodded thoughtfully. "Mike and I talked about it, too," she said. "Let him know what you have in mind, and he can start getting construction bids from the local contractors."

Christina waited impatiently for a break in her mother's conversation with George. Finally Ashleigh turned to her. "Did you need something?" she asked.

"Can I borrow your car?" Christina asked. "I need to run into Lexington, and Melanie has the Blazer."

"Sure," Ashleigh said. "The keys are hanging on the key rack in the kitchen. When will you be home?"

"I don't know," Christina said as she headed out the door. "I have some shopping to do."

As she drove to town she mentally ran through a list of the stores where she might be able to find what she wanted to get for Melanie.

She spent what seemed like hours wandering

through the shopping mall at the edge of town, but by the time she had gone through every store in the mall, she hadn't been able to find the special gift she had in mind. As she left the mall, feeling like a failure, she noticed a small store advertising original artwork. She parked on the street and hurried to the door. When she saw a bronze bust of a Thoroughbred, the mane windswept and the details so perfect she could almost see the look of eagles in the statue's eye, she drew in a sharp breath. "Perfect," she exclaimed. She might not be able to get through to Melanie with words, but she hoped the statue would remind Melanie of what they both loved most about working with the horses. Maybe then Melanie would realize that caring about the Thoroughbreds was the most important thing to Christina, too.

The price on the piece made her gulp, but Christina knew it was worth every penny, and soon she was carrying her purchase to the car, filled with hope that the gift would break the deadlock between her and Melanie.

When she arrived at Whitebrook, her father's pickup was gone and Ian was waiting for her at the house. "Where is everyone?" Christina asked him.

"Melanie's been in an accident," he said tensely.

Christina gasped. "Is she all right?"

"I don't know," Ian said, looking worried. "Your

parents went to the hospital. I've been waiting for you to get back—I'll drive you over there now."

Trembling with worry, Christina climbed into Ian's car, still holding the box with the statue. She stared out the window during the drive, her thoughts only of Melanie. Her cousin had to be all right. How could so many bad things be happening to everyone she cared about?

When they arrived at the hospital Christina leaped from the car as soon as Ian stopped it at the main entrance. "I'll be in as soon as I find a parking place," he said. Christina nodded and slammed the door shut, then dashed through the hospital's automatic doors and hurried down the hall, the box with the statue still in her hands. She stopped when she saw her parents sitting in the emergency room waiting area.

Ashleigh stood up. "The doctor is still with Melanie," she told Christina. "We're waiting for him to come out. But she's conscious, and so far it doesn't seem like there are any major injuries."

Christina sank into a vinyl chair beside her father and gripped the gift box with both hands. "Do you know anything else?"

Mike reached over to give Christina's white-knuckled hand a squeeze. "She just got back from getting X rays, and they're getting her settled in her room."

Ashleigh sat down again and leaned back in the chair. Christina looked anxiously at her mother, whose face was pale, her expression anxious.

"Are you all right?" Mike asked Ashleigh.

Ashleigh nodded. "I know Melanie's okay," she said. "But I guess I'm still shaken from getting that phone call."

Christina sat on the edge of her seat, clutching the box. As relieved as she was to discover that Melanie's injuries were nothing life-threatening, she knew that there were other important concerns. What if Melanie was too badly hurt to be able to race again? Melanie lived for the track and for her horses. Christina swallowed down a lump of fear and waited impatiently for the doctor to talk to them. She watched the second hand on the old-fashioned clock creep around the face. Every minute seemed like an hour.

After what felt like an eternity a doctor came into the waiting area and stopped in front of Mike, Ashleigh, and Christina. "Melanie has a mild concussion and some bumps and bruises," he told them. "We want to keep her for a day or so for observation, but I'm sure she's going to bounce back without any side effects."

"Thank you," Mike said, the relief obvious in his voice. "When can we see her?"

"Right away," the doctor said, giving them Melanie's room number before he left.

"Your mother and I will go find Ian," Mike said, rising. "You can go talk to Melanie first."

Christina walked slowly down the hall, wondering what she and Melanie would say to each other. When she reached Melanie's room, she hesitated in the doorway, her breath caught in her chest. Melanie's head was bandaged, and her face was covered with scratches. She looked small and frail in the hospital bed, and Christina's heart clenched at the sight. Melanie's face was turned toward the window.

A sudden panic filled Christina. She didn't know what to say to her cousin. What if Melanie was still upset with her? What if now she blamed Christina for the car accident as well, since they'd fought right before she drove off? Or maybe Melanie understood now how easy it was to let something bad happen when you had something else on your mind that really mattered to you.

After a moment Melanie turned her head to face Christina. Her eyes widened and she took a deep breath, but she didn't say anything.

Christina couldn't tell what her cousin was thinking from the look on her face—was she still angry? Too shocked from the accident to talk? Now wasn't the best time to talk about Raven, but Christina just needed Melanie to know how much she meant to her.

"I brought you something," she said, stepping inside the room to set the box on the bedside table. "I'm glad you're okay."

Melanie bit her lip, then turned her head away again. Christina stood there awkwardly for a moment, then let out a small sigh and left the room.

When she reached the waiting area, Ian, Mike, and Ashleigh were there, talking in low voices.

"You guys go ahead and see Melanie," Christina told her parents. "I'm going back home."

Ian gazed at her for a second, then nodded in understanding. "I'll drive you," he said.

When they reached Whitebrook, Christina went straight to the barn. She stopped at Raven's stall. The sling was twisted a little, and Christina stepped inside to straighten the strap. As she did she noticed that a patch of Raven's black coat had rubbed off along the edge of the sling. Christina stroked the filly's neck gently. "You and Melanie both have to get better now," she said. Raven twisted her head back to bite at the sling. Christina wondered how much longer it would be until Dr. Seymour would let Raven try to walk.

Raven made a move to kick out with her good leg, trying to break loose of the restraint, and Christina stroked her shoulder, trying to calm the agitated horse. "You can't take much more of this, can you?" Christina asked.

Raven tossed her head and struck out again with her leg, expressing her frustration the best she could.

"How's she doing?" Ian walked up to the stall and looked in at Raven.

"Not very good," Christina said sadly.

"I'll give her a dose of the sedative Dr. Seymour left," Ian said. He headed for the office to get the medication, and Christina left the barn, hating the feeling of helplessness that filled her. There didn't seem to be anything she could do to help Raven—or to make things better with Melanie.

11

"That should help you calm down a bit," Ashleigh said after Ian gave Raven a dose of sedative. Raven made another feeble attempt to free herself from the sling, but the medication worked quickly, and soon she was quiet. Ashleigh watched for several minutes, making sure the filly was relaxed before she went back to her office.

She sat at the desk and started sorting through a stack of unopened mail, thinking about Christina and Melanie and how to help the two girls she loved so much. Both of them were obviously so anxious about the upcoming Derby that it was leading to serious danger—first Christina's wreck with Raven, and now Melanie's car accident. She needed to find a way to calm their nerves before anyone else got hurt. But what was the answer?

When Ashleigh unearthed the latest *Daily Racing Form*, she set the rest of the mail aside and scanned the front page, happy for the distraction.

"Celtic Mist Is Townsend Acres' Derby Hopeful," the front-page headline read. Below the article was a grainy black-and-white photo showing the colt galloping on the track. Ashleigh glanced through the article, which was full of quotes by Brad Townsend boasting about his colt and about Townsend Acres' many successes. She started to set the paper aside, but the name Wonder's Pride caught her attention.

She reread the article carefully, slowing when she reached the part that mentioned Pride.

"Townsend Acres has always strived to train for excellence," Brad was quoted as saying. "Our one big failure was to let a teenage jockey and a geriatric trainer control Wonder's Pride in his bid for the Triple Crown. Pride would have been one of our greatest success stories if it hadn't been for the inferior work done by other people."

Ashleigh felt her jaw tighten. She crumpled the paper into a wad and threw it in the trash can, seething at Brad's outrageous statement. She hadn't thought it was possible, but Brad seemed to get more intolerable by the day.

She looked up at the photos of Pride on the office wall and remembered Charlie's distress about the colt's condition and how Samantha had worried herself sick over Pride's well-being. There had been nothing inferior about the work they had done with Pride to keep him in top form.

She could hear Charlie again, fretting over Pride and trying to keep the colt healthy enough to handle his overwhelming race schedule. . . .

"I think we should skip the Belmont," Charlie said flatly. He was standing with Ashleigh and Samantha outside Pride's stall. The colt, who had run so magnificently just three days before, looked as though he could hardly get his nose up to his hay net.

Ashleigh pinched her lips together and glanced at Samantha. The slender redhead frowned as she gazed at her beloved Pride. "He deserves better than being run to death just because Brad has his father convinced that it's in Townsend Acres' best interest. All Brad wants is to take credit for his success," Samantha said bitterly.

"But to withdraw now would take away his chance to go down in glory as a Triple Crown winner," Ashleigh protested. "We still have a couple of weeks to get him rested."

"He can't run the way he has been," Charlie said.

"He needs to rest for several months, not days."

"We don't have months," Ashleigh said. She knew Charlie was right, but after just one more race, Pride could have all the rest he needed. "Besides," she added, "if we withdraw, Brad will convince Clay that they need to take over, and they'll race him anyway, with or without me on him."

Charlie grunted in disgust. "You're right, but I still don't think it's reasonable to push the colt as hard as he's been pushed and expect him to stay on top."

"What can we do?" Samantha asked.

"We'll race him," Charlie said sourly. "But," he added, looking at Ashleigh, "don't expect anything great from him. This colt is completely run out as far as I can see."

Samantha gazed at the exhausted animal. "I'll do everything I can for him," she promised, not sounding very sure of herself.

But after two weeks of pampering and easy works, Pride still hadn't regained his full strength. They arrived in New York for the Belmont, not sure that Pride would be ready to run in the famous third jewel of the Triple Crown. His weight was still down, but to Ashleigh's relief, he seemed to have recovered at least some of his spirit and fire.

"You've worked wonders with him," Ashleigh told

Samantha as they stood outside Pride's stall at the Belmont track. Pride had his head poked into the aisle and was looking around, his eyes bright with excitement. "He's going to be great for the race. I'm sure he can handle it, Sammy."

"I hope so," Samantha replied, rubbing Pride's nose gently. "I just wish we had more time for him to recover."

On Saturday morning Ashleigh helped Samantha prepare Pride for the race. Samantha spent extra time grooming his coat until it glistened in the sun.

"Just don't force him," Charlie said sternly, running his hand down Pride's cannon as he frowned up at Ashleigh, who was combing the colt's mane. "If he doesn't feel like he's got the drive to keep up the pace, let him off easy, Ashleigh."

Ashleigh nodded, wiping a bead of sweat from her forehead. The heat in New York was bothering her, and she knew it had to be stressing Pride as well. She'd have liked to have an easy race, but it was impossible with the field of horses they'd be running against that day. And the pressure from the Townsends weighed heavily on her. If Pride didn't do well, there would be some big problems with Clay and Brad, and she would do anything she could to avoid that. Besides, if Pride won the Belmont, he would never have to set hoof on a track again. Holding the Triple Crown would ensure his value as a prized stallion, and Clay Townsend couldn't ask for more than that.

When they rode onto the track for the post parade, Pride danced a little alongside the pony horse, and Ashleigh patted his neck, frowning as she felt the sweat that already dampened his neck. "Attaboy," she said softly. "We're going to do a great job today, aren't we?"

When the starting bell drove them from the number ten slot, Ashleigh held Pride back, staying in fourth place, even though it infuriated the colt to see horses ahead of him on the track. Count Abdul, the colt that had pushed Pride into a speed duel in the Kentucky Derby, held the lead.

"Rate yourself, fellow," she told the colt. "We have a mile and a half to run here. Let's save some for the end." But Pride tugged at her, obviously wanting to go. When another colt passed them, Ashleigh could feel Pride straining to keep up the pace, and she knew she had to let him run, even though she was worried about him tiring himself out.

"You have so much heart," she said, awed by Pride's tenacity and spirit. Pride kept pressing forward, focused on the horses that were running ahead of them, and Ashleigh let the determined colt make his move. He stretched out, driving past Count Abdul.

Ashleigh glanced behind when they reached the half-mile marker. "We're ahead by two lengths!" she called to Pride. "We're going to do this, boy!"

They neared the pole marking the sixteenth furlong when suddenly another colt came up beside them. Pride flattened his ears against his head and dug into the track, straining to keep up the pace. Ashleigh kneaded her fisted hands along his neck, urging Pride on, but she could tell he didn't have the reserves of energy that had carried him through the Derby and the Preakness.

The colt's sweat-soaked neck and harsh breathing worried Ashleigh, but she could see the finish line ahead of them, and she let Pride run his fastest as Super Value, the challenger, moved ahead by a nose.

"We can do this," Ashleigh called, encouraging the weary colt to give a little more. But when it came down to the wire, Pride took second by a nose bob. Ashleigh felt sick with disappointment, but even more, she worried about Pride, whose labored breathing continued even after they led him to the backside to cool him out.

"You were incredible," she told Pride as Samantha slowly walked him out.

"He ran his heart out," Charlie agreed. "But you can only ask so much of an animal. Pride's given his best."

• • •

The slamming of a car door drew Ashleigh back to the present. She rose from her desk to see who had come to visit.

"Is anybody home?" she heard Samantha Nelson call, and a few seconds later Ian's red-haired daughter strode into the office.

"Hi there, stranger," Samantha said with a grin. "I was on my way to town and the car just decided to turn up your driveway."

"I haven't seen you for ages," Ashleigh said, coming around the desk to give Samantha a quick hug. "How are things at Whisperwood?"

"Tor and I have been so busy with lessons and training that I barely have time to eat and sleep," Samantha said, smiling. "But I'm doing what I love, so I can't complain."

Ashleigh nodded in understanding.

Samantha frowned at her. "You look a little stressed," she commented. "Is there something going on that I should know about?"

Ashleigh sat down at the desk again and forced a smile. "Chris and Melanie are both so overwrought about the Derby that they can't think straight," she said.

"Dad told me about Raven and Melanie," Samantha said. "How are they doing now?"

"It'll still be a while before we know for sure about Raven," Ashleigh replied. "But Melanie's going to be fine once she recovers from some minor injuries. I just wish the girls would listen when I explain that they have to take it easy. Chris doesn't seem to think I know what I'm doing when it comes to Star's training."

Samantha wrinkled her nose. "I know how you feel. I remember wishing people would listen to me when we were working with Pride," she said. "I understood him better than anyone, but the Townsends never gave me any credit for knowing what I was talking about."

Ashleigh nodded. "That's exactly what I'm talking about," she said. "I just keep thinking about what happened with Pride, and I don't want to see Star end up the same way."

Samantha cocked her head to the side. "Ash, you do know that things were very different for Pride than they are now for Star, right?" she pointed out. "And Chris certainly knows her horse well."

Ashleigh frowned. "So you think I could be wrong?" she asked.

Samantha shrugged. "Maybe Chris really does know what he needs," she said. "Just think about it."

After Samantha left, Ashleigh stayed at her desk, looking at the photo of her on Pride at Churchill

Downs. Then her gaze drifted to the picture of Christina on Star. Maybe Samantha was right, she thought. What if she was letting her own worries keep her from seeing how well Christina understood what Star needed? She hadn't helped Christina's confidence a bit by not giving her some credit for knowing her own horse better than anyone else. But it was too late now to schedule a race for Star before the Derby. Ashleigh sank back in her chair and gnawed at her lower lip. What was she going to do?

12

"Okay, Chris," Ashleigh said. "I want you to take Star around the track at a slow gallop today. Tomorrow we'll take the speed up a notch, then we'll wait a couple of days and breeze him."

Ashleigh released the hold she had on Star's bridle, and Christina guided the energized colt onto the practice track, feeling the same excitement he did. She concentrated on staying relaxed, trying to keep her own anticipation from getting Star more worked up than he already was.

Melanie stood at the rail, clearly frustrated about being on the sidelines. Because of her concussion, she still had to wait a few more days before she could ride again. They hadn't really talked since Melanie had come back from the hospital, but she didn't seem as angry anymore. Christina wondered if her gift, along with the shock of the car accident, had finally melted her cousin's stubborn irritation. But there still remained an awkwardness between them—a tension in the air. Christina glanced in her direction now, and Melanie quickly looked down at her hands, avoiding eye contact.

Christina turned her attention to Star, walking him briskly along the outside rail. He felt strong beneath her, and she knew he was eager to run. After a lap she moved him into a jog but kept him under tight rein, not wanting the colt to burst into a gallop and pull a muscle. After a couple more laps around the track, she laid a hand on his shoulder and felt the heat starting to radiate from him. She looked at Ashleigh, who was standing at the rail next to Melanie.

"Go ahead and gallop," Ashleigh called, and Christina urged Star to speed up. He snorted and tossed his head, then settled into a powerful gallop that made Christina's heart race.

"You still have it," she told the colt as they moved around the oval. Even at an easy pace she could feel the strength in his strides, and she wanted to let him break into a hard run as much as she felt he wanted to do it.

"Tomorrow," she told the eager colt, keeping a strong grip on the reins. "You'll get to do more then, all right?"

When they finished the gallop, Star had only broken a light sweat and was breathing easily. Christina slowed him to a jog for another lap, then rode him off the track, unable to keep from grinning broadly.

"He's in perfect shape," she told Ashleigh, who was nodding in satisfaction. Christina looked where Melanie had been standing before, but she was gone.

"He sure looks good," Ashleigh agreed, making some notes on the clipboard she held. "You both looked great out there, Chris." She caught the colt's bridle as Christina swung off Star's back and pulled his saddle from his back.

Christina moved her gaze beyond her mother and noticed Melanie leading Image toward the track, tacked up and ready to ride. Christina raised her eyebrows at her cousin. "You aren't supposed to—"

"I know," Melanie interrupted her. "But you can work her for me."

Christina looked from Melanie to Image. "Are you sure?" she asked, stunned by her cousin's offer. No one but Melanie rode Image.

"I'm going to go crazy not being able to ride for a few more days," Melanie admitted. "But she needs to be worked." She looked into Christina's eyes, and Christina could feel the silent message there—a question about their friendship. "Would you mind exercising her for me?"

"I'd be glad to," Christina said, her heart swelling with happiness. As she swung onto Image's back she felt as though another weight had been lifted off her. "Tell me what you want me to do."

Melanie gave her a small smile. "I think you know what to do," she said.

Once they were on the track, Christina glanced at Melanie, who was watching them closely. Christina tried to handle Image the way she had seen Melanie do, keeping her full attention on the filly.

Although Image fought the strange rider at first, soon she settled down and began moving around the track at a steady pace. Christina began to relax a little. They made several circuits of the track as Christina concentrated on listening to the filly, figuring out how best to communicate with her.

Soon she moved Image into a gallop, paying close attention to how she moved. The power and length of the filly's strides made Christina realize how much competition Image was going to be during the Derby. With Melanie jockeying her, the pair was going to be hard to beat. By the time Christina finished exercising Image, she was starting to doubt that she and Star would ever have a chance at winning. When she rode off the track, Melanie and Ashleigh stood waiting together.

"She looks really good," Ashleigh commented, looking from Christina to Melanie.

Melanie nodded, but her expression was serious. "She sure does," she said, then led the filly away without saying anything else.

Christina felt her mood sink. Had she done something wrong while she was riding Melanie's horse? She'd thought things were finally going to get better between them, but now Melanie was acting weird again.

Suddenly Dani burst from the barn doorway, waving her arms frantically. "Raven's out of her sling!" the groom exclaimed.

Melanie froze, and Ashleigh and Christina stared at each other for a split second. As Dani hurried out to take Image from Melanie, Christina and Ashleigh dashed toward the barn.

Melanie passed them in the aisle, running as fast as she could to Raven's stall. When Christina reached the stall, Melanie was already inside, trying to hold the filly's injured leg up. But Raven pulled it away and planted it firmly on the ground, as if to say she would have no more nonsense of not being able to stand on her own four legs. The filly had managed to wrench the sling from the hooks Mike and Ian had put in the beam over her stall, and the canvas strip was trampled into the bedding.

"I called Dr. Seymour," Ian said when he reached the stall. He gazed at Raven. "I guess she's trying to tell us she's ready for a change."

Christina caught the look he and Ashleigh gave each other, and a sense of foreboding came over her. What if this was too soon? If Raven had reinjured herself, she knew that it would be the end for the filly. She slipped into the stall to help Melanie keep Raven still until Dr. Seymour arrived.

While they waited for the vet, Christina and Melanie kept their attention on Raven, neither of them speaking directly to each other.

"Hold still, girl," Melanie begged the agitated filly. "Have a little more patience."

"You're fine," Christina crooned to Raven. "You just need to stand quietly, okay?"

It was almost half an hour before Dr. Seymour got to the farm. When he reached Raven's stall, he shook his head. "I was afraid she would do something like this," he said, eyeing the ruined sling. "She was getting tired of being stuck in here." He opened the stall door. "Bring her out," he said, sounding resigned.

Melanie led Raven into the aisle. The filly took slow, cautious steps, but in spite of her trembling muscles, she walked steadily. Dr. Seymour did a careful examination of her leg, then rose, dusting his hands on his pants. "She seems to be doing better," he said.

At Melanie's gasp of joy, he frowned. "I said she's better, not perfect," he said firmly.

"Will she be all right to breed?" Ashleigh asked quickly.

Dr. Seymour gazed thoughtfully at Raven. "She has excellent conformation," he said. "I think she'll do great as a broodmare."

Christina expelled a sigh of relief.

"I can hardly wait to see what kinds of foals she produces," Melanie said.

"Me too," Mike said. "I think we should plan on breeding her to Pride in a year."

Melanie ran a hand along Raven's neck. "You'll have the most beautiful foal Whitebrook ever saw," she told the filly.

"For the time being," Dr. Seymour said, "I want her kept in the stall with short walks on a lead to rebuild her muscles."

"I'll take care of her," Christina and Melanie said at the same time. They looked at each other, and Christina gave her cousin a cautious smile. When Melanie smiled back, Christina sighed with relief.

After the vet left the farm, Christina busied herself cleaning Raven's stall. When she was done, she found Melanie at Image's stall, grooming the black filly.

"How is she doing?" Christina asked.

"She's fine," Melanie said. She stopped brushing Image and looked hard at her cousin.

"Then what's wrong?" Christina asked.

"It's just . . . you made her look so great this morning," Melanie admitted. "I started to think that I'm not a good enough jockey to race her in the Derby."

"What?" Christina exclaimed. "You and Image are incredible together, Mel. When I was riding her I was thinking that Star and I could hardly compete against the two of you. She's an awesome filly, and she's going to burn up the track at Churchill Downs."

"I hope so," Melanie replied. "But you and Star are going to be hard to beat." She returned to grooming Image, and Christina left the barn. She stopped short when she got outside. Parker's pickup truck was coming up the driveway. She folded her arms across her chest and watched him drive up to the barn.

When Parker pulled to a stop, Christina realized he wasn't alone in the truck. The curly-haired girl he had been with at the track was sitting in the passenger seat. Christina felt her jaw sag. Didn't Parker care about her at all? Did he think it wouldn't bother her if he brought his new girlfriend to Whitebrook?

Parker hopped out of the truck and gave her a friendly wave. Christina stood still, waiting for him to say something.

"You look great," Parker said, giving her a warm smile.

Christina felt herself melt, despite everything. "It hasn't been that long since you've seen me," she said. "I haven't changed much."

"I saw you leaving Keeneland the other day," Parker said. "Why didn't you stick around to talk?"

"I was in a bit of a hurry," Christina said, surprised that Parker would have wanted her to meet his new girlfriend.

"But there's someone I wanted to introduce to you," Parker said. He gestured at the girl in the truck. "Kirsten was really disappointed that she didn't get a chance to talk to you at the track."

When she climbed out of the truck, the girl looked around the farm, then gave Christina a huge smile. "This place is really beautiful," she said. "You are so lucky to live on a Thoroughbred farm. Parker told me all about how you saved your colt and now you're going to race him in the Kentucky Derby. I could hardly wait to meet you."

Christina was torn. How could she dislike someone who was so friendly? But how could she like Parker's replacement girlfriend? She forced a smile. "It *is* really nice here," she said. "But the Townsends have a magnificent farm. We don't have nearly as nice a facility as they do."

The girl sniffed. "I like your place much better," she said. "Townsend Acres is a little too snooty for my taste."

Christina choked back a laugh, but Parker roared.

"You always say just what you think, don't you, Kirsten?"

She grinned and nodded. "It really ticks Uncle Brad off," she said.

Christina stared at the girl, her mouth going dry. "Uncle Brad?" she echoed.

Parker nodded. "If you had stayed a little longer at Keeneland, you could have met my cousin then."

Christina felt the ice around her heart melt completely.

"Can we see Star?" Kirsten asked.

Christina nodded happily. "Sure. Follow me."

Giddy with excitement over discovering that Kirsten was just Parker's cousin, she practically skipped as she led them to Star's paddock. Star came to the fence immediately, whinnying a greeting as he crossed the pasture.

"He is so beautiful," Kirsten said breathlessly, reaching out to let Star snuffle at her fingers. She glanced at Parker. "And a lot more friendly than that

Celtic Mist Uncle Brad keeps bragging about." She glanced at Christina. "I'll bet he is really something to watch on the track."

"He is," Parker said emphatically. "And you should see Chris ride. You'd never know she's only been a jockey for a year."

Kirsten grinned at Christina. "Parker told me how you two sneaked off with a racehorse to get your license. That took a lot of guts."

Christina winced at the memory. "I thought my parents were going to ground me for life after that little stunt," she admitted.

"But you did what you set out to do," Parker reminded her. "And that's what's going to happen at the Derby. You and Star can't be beat, Chris. You know you'll be riding a winner, and Star has the best jockey I've ever met."

"Thanks," Christina said, feeling herself blush at the praise.

After Parker and Kirsten left, Christina climbed into Star's paddock and gave the colt some carrot bits she had in her jeans pocket. "Everything seems to be working out okay, boy," she said as Star nuzzled her hands, searching for more treats. "But I'm still worried about the Derby."

"Why?"

Christina snapped her head around to see Ashleigh standing at the fence.

"Uh, hi, Mom. I was just talking to Star."

Ashleigh nodded. "I used to spend a lot of time talking to Wonder, too," she said. "I could talk to her about things that I couldn't tell anyone else."

Christina didn't say anything, but Ashleigh stayed by the rail. "I know you can talk to Star, but can you tell me what has you so worried about the race? Is it because of what happened with Raven?"

Christina took a deep breath. "No, it's not that," she said. "Cindy helped me see that I couldn't let that stop me from giving Star his chance. But I'm worried about how well we'll do. I really want the best for Melanie and Image, but more than anything, I want Star to live up to the legacy Wonder, Pride, and Champion have left for him."

"I understand," Ashleigh said, leaning over the fence to rub Star's nose. "And I owe you an apology."

"For what?" Christina asked, surprised.

"I was afraid to let Star be himself," Ashleigh confessed. "Every time I see him on the track, I'm seeing Pride again. I keep thinking of how exhausted Pride was. I didn't want the same thing to happen with Star. I'd love to see him win the Triple Crown, but I wasn't being fair to you and him. You're right, Chris. You know Star better than anyone else, and I should have listened to you, too."

Christina felt more pressure being lifted from her, and she smiled at her mother. "I should have trusted your experience more, too."

"So now that we've got that cleared up, how about scheduling a race for Star?"

Christina stared at Ashleigh. "But the Derby is only a couple of weeks away now. By the time we get him entered in another race, it'll be too close."

"I have something else in mind," Ashleigh said with a grin.

"What?" Christina felt curiosity bubbling up inside her. "How are you going to get him into a race at the last minute?"

"Just wait," Ashleigh said mysteriously. "You'll see."

13

"You guys look great!" Christina stood at the rail of the Whitebrook track while Melanie jogged Image around the oval. Her parents and Ian stood by the rail near Christina, watching the pair closely. Melanie was finally riding again after her forced layoff, and the look of bliss on her face made Christina smile.

Christina still wasn't sure why Ashleigh had asked her and Melanie to wait until late in the morning to work Image and Star, but she was sure her mother had a good reason. She would just have to be patient to find out what that reason was.

The sun warmed the air, and Christina, dressed in jeans and a light T-shirt, closed her eyes for a moment, enjoying the balmy weather. The fresh air mingled with the horsy scents of the farm, and she inhaled deeply.

"Hey, Chris," Melanie called. "Check this out!"

Christina opened her eyes to see Melanie crouch over Image's withers and move the filly into a slow gallop. Melanie guided Image along the inside rail, her hands fisted against Image's shiny black neck.

"Go, Mel!" she called, admiring Image's powerful strides as they galloped by.

"They both look good and ready for the big race," Ian commented as Melanie and Image galloped into the turn.

Ashleigh nodded, watching the horse and rider closely. "It's going to be quite a day at Churchill Downs," she said. "I'm looking forward to it."

"Me too," Christina said.

"And with any luck we'll have two more memorable days at Pimlico and Belmont," Ian said.

"Only time will tell," Ashleigh said. "Remember how we thought Pride could make it through all three races?"

Ian scowled. "He would have if it hadn't been for the Townsends pushing so hard."

"It wasn't all their fault," Ashleigh said quickly. "I got so wrapped up with the stress over the races that I let Pride down, too." She glanced at Christina and smiled. "Sometimes it's hard to remember what's important when there's so much pressure on you."

Christina nodded in agreement. She knew she would never forget that lesson. The horses and the people in her life were way more important than any race could ever be.

"It took Samantha to get me back on track," Ashleigh said. "If it hadn't been for her stepping in and insisting that what Pride needed was peace and rest so that he could run well, he never would have come back to win the Jockey Club Gold Cup after so many bad races."

Ian smiled fondly when Ashleigh mentioned his older daughter. "She does have good horse sense," he said, then looked from Ashleigh to Christina. "Much like two other people I know."

"Where is Sammy today?" Ashleigh asked. "I thought she was going to be here."

"She wanted to," Ian said. "But she and Tor had a jumping clinic scheduled. Otherwise I'm sure she wouldn't have missed this for the world."

Christina started to ask what Samantha and her husband, Tor Nelson, wouldn't miss, but the sound of a vehicle coming up the drive distracted her. She looked over her shoulder to see Ben al-Rihani's sedan pulling up to the barn. As Tall Oaks' owner parked near the track, Parker's pickup turned up the drive-way.

What was Parker doing at Whitebrook when he had horses to prepare for his part on the Olympic equestrian team?

"Are we having a party that I didn't know about?" Christina asked her mother.

"You'll see," Ashleigh said vaguely.

Ben and Cindy got out of the car and walked toward the rail of the practice track. *They make a cute couple*, Christina thought. Ben, tall and dignified-looking in dark slacks and a white shirt, towered over petite, blond Cindy, who was wearing jeans and a tank top.

Christina was even more surprised when Dani brought Star out of the barn, followed by Kevin McLean, who was leading Catwink. Both horses were tacked up and ready to ride.

"What's going on?" Christina demanded, frowning in confusion at her mother.

Ben and Cindy reached them before Ashleigh had a chance to answer.

"I'm glad you could make it," Ashleigh said, giving the retired jockey a quick hug. "It's good to see you, too, Ben." Ashleigh greeted the handsome stable owner with a warm handshake. "How are things going with the new farm? I hear Tall Oaks is going to have a pretty good showing at the Derby. Gratis's published works have been very impressive."

Ben smiled broadly, then looked at Cindy. "My partner has everything running like clockwork," he said. "She's got Gratis more than ready for the Derby."

Cindy looked at Christina. "I only wish we had his best jockey to race him," she said.

"Sorry," Christina said, reaching out to pet Star while Dani held him near the track. "I have my own winner to race this year."

As Image jogged by, Star snorted and tossed his head, tugging at the hold the groom had on his bridle. He struck the ground impatiently, craning his neck to watch Image as Melanie took the filly around the track again.

"You must be excited to have a horse running this year," Ian commented.

"We are," Ben replied. "This truly is a dream come true for me."

"Will your father come over from Dubai to watch the race?" Ashleigh asked. Ben's father had been breeding Thoroughbreds in Saudi Arabia for several years. It had always been his dream to have one of his own horses run in the Triple Crown series, but the races were limited to American-bred horses.

Ben shook his head. "My father's failing health

keeps him from traveling much anymore," he said. "But both Father and Mother are very excited about seeing an al-Rihani horse in the Kentucky Derby, so they'll be glued to the television set for the race."

"Are we too late?" Parker asked as he and Kirsten hurried to the track.

"We haven't missed anything, have we?" Kirsten asked Ashleigh.

"What is she talking about?" Christina was completely mystified. Everyone around her seemed to know what was going on, but she was in the dark.

"You're just in time," Ashleigh replied, ignoring Christina's question.

"In time for what?" Christina demanded.

Instead of answering her, Ashleigh turned to Ben and Cindy again.

Kirsten focused her attention on Star. "I brought him some carrots," she told Christina. "May I feed them to him later?"

"Of course," Christina said. "He loves attention, and he loves attention with treats even more."

Star angled his head toward Kirsten, who stroked his long nose. "You are the most handsome horse in the world," she crooned to him.

"He knows," Christina said, laughing as Star tossed his head, as though showing off his elegant profile.

Parker grinned at Christina. "I'm looking forward to seeing a Whitebrook horse and jockey in the Kentucky Derby," he said. "I wasn't even born when Pride raced, and I wasn't old enough to remember Champion running."

"I'm excited, too," Kirsten said, still petting Star while Dani held the colt. "But I'll be watching it on television, since I'm leaving for home tomorrow." She smiled at Ashleigh. "Thanks for inviting me today."

"You'd better get Star on the track," Dani said, moving the colt so that Christina could mount up. Star had his attention fixed on Image, who was cantering easily around the oval. Every time the black filly moved away from them, Star started prancing in place, clearly impatient to get on the track.

"Are you sure you want us to share the track with Melanie and Image?" Christina asked Ashleigh.

Ashleigh nodded. "I think it's exactly what Star needs," she said. "I told you I'd find a way to arrange a race for you and Star."

"With only two horses?" Christina asked as she swung onto Star's back and looked onto the track. Melanie was jogging Image again, keeping the filly warm.

"Three," Dani said, pulling her helmet onto her head. "I get to ride Catwink." She grinned at Christina.

"I know we won't be much of a threat to Star and Image, especially with me on board. But we'll do our best to keep the competition hot for you."

As Christina rode Star onto the track, the colt scooted sideways, expressing his eagerness to run. Christina held him in, forcing him to hold a steady jog for several laps, moving in the opposite direction of Image. In a few minutes Dani joined her, and soon Star and Catwink were warmed up.

Christina stopped at the rail, where her parents and Ian were visiting with Ben and Cindy. Parker and Kirsten were talking with Kevin.

"What kind of race did you have in mind?" she asked.

Ashleigh smiled up at her. "We'll do an old-fashioned standing start without using the gate," she said. "I want to see the three of you run six furlongs."

"Okay," Christina said slowly, not quite convinced that this mock race was going to be the same thing as a real race for Star.

"It's the closest thing to a race I could put together at this point," Ashleigh said, offering her an apologetic smile. "Do you think Star will be disappointed?"

Christina knew that by giving her a chance to race Star, even in a small way, her mother was trying to tell her that she trusted Christina's instincts about the colt.

Christina gave her mother a confident smile. "Star,

disappointed about racing? No way!" Christina circled Star to the spot where the practice gate was normally set up, joining Melanie and Dani on their mounts.

She lined Star up between Image and Catwink and held the colt steady, waiting for Ian to cue them to start running. The three horses shifted, dancing in place, fighting their riders to let them do what they loved— run like the wind. Christina leaned forward onto Star's shoulders, feeling the same mounting tension that filled her at the start of every race. "We can do this, boy," she murmured to Star. "Let's show them all how great a runner you are."

Star flicked his ears back and stamped the ground, bouncing his hindquarters a little to show that he was more than ready to race.

When Ian's hand finally came down as a signal to go, it took Christina little urging to get Star into a full gallop, with Catwink and Image breaking into a run on either side of him.

Star's ears flicked back and forth as he assessed the competition, but Christina kept her eyes forward, focused on the track ahead of them. She could feel Image close by her side, and she hunched forward, kneading her fists up Star's neck.

"Let's go," she said to the colt, and Star stretched out a little, moving slightly ahead of Image and Catwink.

Dani held the gray filly to a good pace, but Christina knew her real threat came from Melanie and Image. As they came into the turn Image pulled ahead of Star, stretching her long neck and digging hard into the packed footing of the track.

To Christina's dismay, Image put on a sudden burst of speed and shot past them. Star flattened his ears as the filly's black hip passed his nose. Melanie moved Image toward the rail, trying to save track as they thundered along the backstretch.

"We can't let them get away with that!" Christina cried to Star, edging him closer to the inside rail. As they raced toward the turn she was aware of Catwink close on her right side.

"Let's get them," Christina told her galloping colt, crouching over his shoulders. Image was close to the rail, but Christina could see enough of a gap to allow them to shoot through and win the race neatly. But as they drew near the rail Christina thought of Raven and how quickly the wreck had happened. She couldn't risk that again. She held Star back a little, then asked him for more speed. The colt dug in, moved up another gear, and neatly maneuvered between Catwink and Image, pulling up on Image's hip.

"That's it, boy!" Christina cried, asking Star for more speed. The colt responded by lengthening his strides and stretching his nose forward. Christina was awed by the power and strength Star displayed, tearing toward the finish line with ground-eating strides.

As they came up beside Image, Melanie glanced beside her, her face registering surprise to see Star moving up on them so swiftly. She pushed her fists into the filly's neck, urging her to speed up.

Christina did the same with Star, leaning close over his withers as they thundered toward the finish line. Catwink was holding a close third, but Star held his place next to Image and they ran nose to nose for several strides, flashing past the pole that indicated the end of the race.

Christina brought Star to a slow canter, then turned him back toward the group waiting by the rail. The colt was snorting and blowing heavily, but Christina could feel that he still had more to give.

"If it had been a longer race, we would have left you in the dirt," she said to Melanie, laughing.

"Right," Melanie drawled. "Image was just getting started."

"What a great race!" Dani said as she rode up to them, laughing. "That was fun."

"It was too close to call between Star and Image," Ian announced, holding up his stopwatch.

"Hey," Christina said. "Maybe at Churchill Downs we'll have to share the winner's circle."

"We'll have to trim their nose whiskers to the same

length," Ashleigh said. "If the race is that close, it'll be impossible to call."

"Do you think there's room for two horses in the winner's circle?" Melanie joked.

"Lucky for you two, your horses get along," Mike said.

Christina and Melanie glanced at each other.

"Lucky for us, we get along, too," Melanie said, grinning at Christina.

"I hate to spoil all your dreams of the winner's circle," Cindy broke in. "But there's another horse that's going to put some pressure on both of yours. Gratis is going to give you both a run for your money at the track. You two may have to settle for second and third."

"It's going to be an awesome race," Parker said, holding Star while Christina hopped from his back. He grinned at Christina. "I'll be there rooting for White-brook all the way."

"That will get Uncle Brad mad for sure," Kirsten said, laughing. "Especially with Celtic Mist on the track, too."

"Thanks, Parker," Christina said, grateful for his show of loyalty to her and Star.

"It's going to be an unforgettable day, no matter who wins," Ian said.

Christina ran her hand along Star's sleek neck and nodded, imagining herself on Star, posing in the winner's circle at the end of the race. She smiled at the thought but knew there would be lots of tough competition. She and Star still had a lot of work ahead of them if they wanted to win the Derby.

MARY NEWHALL ANDERSON spent her childhood exploring back roads and trails on horseback with her best friend. She now lives with her husband, her horse-crazy daughter, Danielle, and five horses on Washington State's Olympic Peninsula. Mary has published novels and short stories for both adults and young adults.